GAIL PALLOTTA

iii

HIDDEN DANGER

Gail Pallotta

ISBN-13: 978-1-965352-09-0

Acknowledgements

Many thanks to my family for supporting my writing. Their encouragement and suggestions are invaluable. I'm grateful to Sheriff's Deputy Brandon North and Deputy Jon Teusink for helping with police procedures. I couldn't have written the book without their input. Most of all I'm thankful to Jesus, my Lord and Savior, for giving me the words to write *Hidden Danger*.

Chapter One

Emily Hanover jumped and sat straight up in the bed.

She hadn't been dreaming. There it was again, a scraping noise and banging outside the cabin. With a shaky hand she reached for her cell phone and the after-hours number for Larry, the security guard who checked her in at Sky High Campground. She stopped in mid-air. Thinking only of getting her life back together, she'd forgotten to charge her phone.

The clanging grew louder, more intense. *You are our only visitor.* Larry had told her. "Few people come to the North Carolina Mountains in January and February, so the managers take off. Another guard, Nick Lancaster who's on break from college, will be in the office tomorrow."

With a tremor running through her fingers, Emily plugged the phone into the charger. She flinched each time someone hit stone. With what? A shovel. Yes. It banged into a boulder and resounded in the wind howling around the corner of the house.

Quivering, she slid her feet to the floor. Another round of metal met granite. She raised a blind in the bedroom window, stared at the blackness outside, and let the blind drop. She could see no one. Yet, the shovel vibrations echoed. Whoever hit the rock was really angry. She chewed her knuckle. She'd make herself small and hide. She scooted under the covers and shook.

She had traveled here to renew her spirit in these awe-inspiring mountains. After Donnie West dumped her at the altar, she had yearned to rest and regroup at Sky High. A clank rang out, but this time it reverberated inside her. She would no longer lay here and let a trespasser ruin her vacation. She swung her legs over the side of the bed and forced her body up.

She started to turn on the lights. No. She pulled back her hand. Whoever was outside would see her. She snatched pepper spray and a flashlight from the nightstand and started to the country kitchen, nearly dropping the items as she crept down the hall.

Lord, please help me. First, Donnie. Now this. Please help.

As she peered out the small kitchen window over the sink, the shovel blasted into the silence again. She cringed. Only a person up to no good would invade someone else's yard in the middle of the night.

She tiptoed past the dining area and the rock fireplace. Her stomach churned as she crossed the room. Finally, she reached the large sliding glass door in the living area. Careful not to touch the drapes, she peeked out the small crack between two panels. No one was there. Had the person outside left? Hope rippled over her. She waited to make sure though. A man with long hair passed outside on her porch. She yanked the drapes shut as tight as she could.

He carried a body.

With her finger still on the spray cannister, she collapsed to the floor.

~

Emily yawned as her eyelids opened to a new day. Silence. Sweet silence sounded loud as she opened the curtains and watched the sun rise on the mountains towering toward Heaven. A tiny slice of the tranquility she longed for trickled inside her. She let out a sigh of relief and fell asleep.

When she awoke in the afternoon, she looked up as a northern cardinal flew to a naked oak tree and perched on a limb. All seemed right with the world.

But it wasn't.

She hopped up, showered, dressed in jeans and a T-shirt, and left to report last night's incident. With no one else here and only one person in the office, maybe she should go home, but she couldn't. She intended to wash away the shame of standing alone at the altar on her wedding day. When she left, she would take home sweet memories of this beautiful place.

After Donnie created the scene right before Christmas, no less, she'd worked hard to write extra articles for the crime section of "Blue Mountain News" to earn time off to exhale all of her grief. Her friends had told her not to come here because of the risk of getting snowed or iced in. No one had said Sky High Campground was unsafe, not one single person. Anyway, she hadn't even talked to the security guard yet, and the bottom line—she didn't want to leave.

Cold air whipped around her. She picked up her pace and drew close to the office with one question in her head. Could a college student protect her? She darted up the steps with rings of perspiration underneath her arms in spite of the cool mountain air. Apparently, the man at her cabin last night killed some poor person and decided to bury him in her yard until he hit rock digging the grave. Writing about a heinous crime and seeing a person with a dead man were two different things.

She opened the door to the manager's office. An athletic, muscular guy sat behind an old, wooden desk. He looked about twenty-eight, the same age as her, not like a college student. She took a step back. He was strong enough to take care of her if he knew how. He stood, scraping his chair across the wooden, plank floor.

"Hello, ma'am." He glanced at the guest registry. "Miss, uh, Hanover visiting us from Blue Mountain. I'm Nick Lancaster. What can I do for you?"

She wanted to yell "Catch the killer who was outside my cabin last night," but she lost her voice looking into his piercing dark eyes. "Um, there was someone digging outside my cabin last night." Her throat tightened, forcing her to push the next words through it. "I peeped out a crack in the drapes. He carried a dead body over his shoulders."

Nick's face rumpled with doubt.

Oh no, not one of those men who think women are alarmist. Emily wanted to give him a piece of her mind, but what her boss called her natural public relations ability took hold. She tapped the chair in front of his desk. "May I?"

"Yes, of course. Excuse me." He shifted his weight then sat down. "So, tell me why you think someone was in your yard?" He gulped. "With a body." He stretched his neck forward.

Irritated she had to pander to him on so little sleep, heat built inside her and traveled to her cheeks. "I was resting peacefully when all of a sudden in the middle of the night I heard this loud noise." She told him all of the events of the evening while he listened with a blank expression on his face.

"I see." He steepled his fingers. "I can understand how frightening that must've been, but I imagine he was a hunter carrying a deer. You're the only person staying at the campground, but sometimes folks who live around here wander onto our property." He shrugged. "It's the dead of winter."

Dead. He had to use that word?

"There are usually no tourists here this time of the year. Those who come into the woods are simply trying to put food on their tables. We don't mind."

"What do you mean? Who are you talking about?"

"We call them forest people. You know, those who have nowhere else to go. We have caves in these hills that work well for a place to build a fire, wrap up in a blanket, and get a good night's sleep."

He wanted to dismiss the entire dreadful evening as an indigent looking for something to eat. Really? "Well, this man wasn't carrying food, uh, I mean, a deer." She ground her teeth.

He raised his hands then let them fall. "I apologize again. I believe you saw something, or someone. It's simply…well, we're pretty removed from civilization. Most people who visit here are repeat customers who come every year to relax and enjoy themselves. We don't have much crime, occasionally petty theft, or something like that." He drummed his fingers on the desk. "Our guests generally come in the spring, summer, and fall."

It wasn't any of his business why she came in February. Images of wedding guests gasping at her embarrassing moment filled her mind, but he didn't need to know her life story to do his job. She sent him a pointed look.

He rolled the corner of a notepad on his desk. "Let's check it out." He got up and pushed in his chair, its legs grinding against the floor again.

Now they were getting somewhere.

As they walked toward her cabin, the afternoon sun danced on the evergreen foliage. With only a few puffy white clouds hovering over the mountains in the distance, she saw the towering hills in all their majesty. One thing she could count on—they would stay stable no matter what happened in this ever-changing world, and so would Christ. An aura of comfort passed over her. She could trust Jesus no matter how confusing or turbulent her life grew. He remained the same and He still loved her. She was glad she chose this place to nourish her soul and put her back on the path God had selected for her.

She savored the view. With no leaves on the trees the landscape appeared even more expansive than when she visited in the spring. The lush flourish of fall's colorful view had given way to empty spaciousness, revealing the magnitude of God's creation. She could not see an end to the hills filled with hardwoods that looked like skeletons. Nick's voice pulled her away from the scene. "I'm sorry. What did you say?"

"Why did you come here during the winter? It's nice today, but we can have bad weather this time of the year."

She came here because…None of his business. She didn't have to tell him about the Bride's Room. How awful it had been when her mother told her Donnie, who was late, had called and said he would not show up at all. She'd never forget her mother's pained expression. The ache had traveled through her entire body like electricity, and she had collapsed. She'd dated Donnie for two years. She thought she knew him. She trusted him. Her mind fell into a pit the same as it always did when his named popped in it.

"Uh, I asked…"

"Yes, yes." She bit her bottom lip almost drawing blood, but every person she'd invited to the wedding knew. Why not tell this guy? After a few weeks she'd probably never see him again. "I used to come here as a kid with my family and have visited since I started my job in Blue Mountain. I still love this place." She cut her eyes up at him. "One of those repeat customers."

"Got it." He grinned.

"So, so." Just spit it out. "So, my fiancé ended our engagement at the wedding. Since then, I haven't had a chance to do anything except get angry or sad about it. I finally got time off from work and came here to regroup." There, she'd said it. How odd. She'd not been able to say it to her mother and father, or her friends, but she had told a total stranger. Admitting her spirit was injured had freed a tiny piece of dirt from her heart as though the mountain breeze had blown it away.

He nodded. "Hmm. Instead, you found more stress, probably the last thing you need right now."

"Yes." An understated assessment if she'd ever heard one, but she'd let it pass. In minutes he'd see for himself.

He stopped walking. "Here we are. We'll cover the entire yard."

He placed his hand on her back, the touch gentle and comforting. She glanced at his jet, black hair and high cheekbones. His looks attracted her, but so had Donnie's. She waved in the air to swat away the unexpected sensation. As long as he got rid of whoever hauled around the dead body outside her cabin his looks didn't matter. "That's a start, I guess."

~

Whew. Nick needed more caffeine to deal with this lady. Hopefully, soon he'd find a way to prove she witnessed one of the forest people carrying a deer. Surely, if she'd visited here before as she said, she knew wild animals probably turned over her trashcans.

"I'll do the best I can to resolve this. I'm a trained surveillance security guard as well as an armed one, and I was in…in…." He hadn't discussed details of his military service since Caroline. That was three years ago.

"Yes." Emily tapped her foot and looked at him with big anxious eyes.

"I was a military intelligence officer, so I'm pretty good at spotting something suspicious." There, he'd told her without mentioning Caroline. He yearned to return to the office and brew a fresh pot of java, but first he had to convince Miss Hanover she had seen a deer.

Chapter Two

Nick stood in the yard of unit #120 and studied Emily's expression—anxious, possibly fearful. He had his job cut out for him.

He had worked hard to stay on task to finish his studies at Hilltop College in three years. He was almost there. Yet, he needed this position until he graduated. He could've used a little rest after taking exams. But no. He was barely on the clock before he met a woman mistaking a deer for a dead body.

Her big hazel eyes touched him. On top of that, reassuring guests was one of his responsibilities. He had to ease her mind. "Well, I don't see anything out of the ordinary. You're secure at Sky High," he snapped. He cringed. It wasn't Emily's fault he was tired and sleepy. He had to do better. "As I said, don't worry. We'll cover the grounds. I'm here day and night, so you can call me any time." He forced a weak smile.

She lowered her gaze, her long lashes shadowing her cheeks.

He wanted to crawl into a hole at the sound of his half-hearted attempt to convince her everything was fine. Strange though, it was the first real reaction he'd had to a woman since Caroline. Something about Emily struck a tender spot in him. He wouldn't think about that now. He simply needed to do his duty. "We'll get to the bottom of this."

It was nothing but adventurous raccoons after her garbage, but she didn't know that. She was jilted and alone in a deserted campground with lots of empty cabins, just trying to put her life back together. She needed to regroup in a peaceful environment. She had to believe no one carried a dead body outside her cabin. He needed her to know that too. He didn't want a call at midnight or after.

He guided her to the trashcans. Sure enough, they lay on the ground with lots of dirt dug up around them. He pointed to the mess then picked them up. "Look. There probably was an animal out here looking for food."

"I don't see any tracks."

He whistled. There was serious observability underneath her thick, dark lashes. "Of course, the wind last night could've blown away an animal's footprints." He tapped her arm. "Still, we're going to keep inspecting the area."

They continued to the other side of the house and the smell of freshly turned up soil met his nostrils as they rounded the corner. A trench four feet wide, three feet deep, and six feet long lay beside a big boulder. He grasped the Glock 22 at his waist.

"I told you he had a body." Emily pointed at the hollow spot. "Where is it? It's not in that grave."

Uh-oh, now what was he going to say? He had no explanation. "This does look suspicious, but don't get upset. First of all, it's not a grave."

"Not a grave. Then what is it?"

Cleary someone had been digging a hole, but it was only a hole. He couldn't explain it because he didn't know why someone put it there. "I'm not sure, but let's go back to the office. Even though I'm convinced nothing has happened at Sky High, I'm going to call and talk to the sheriff in Broken Arrow to see if they've had any crimes, petty or otherwise."

She nodded. "Thank you."

They pivoted. In a hurry to resolve this situation and get some sleep, Nick strode as fast as he could in the cold wind, pebbles crunching underneath his feet. He glimpsed Emily. A faster walker than most women, she stayed with him step for step.

"How long have you worked at Sky High?" Emily's voice sounded pinched.

Did all women think they needed to make conversation?

The chatter gave her an appearance of bravery. Even though he suspected she rattled on to cover up her anxiety, he wanted to make sure she stayed strong. He would contribute to the chat as best he could on so little rack time.

"When I decided to go to college, I landed the job here to supplement my G. I. loan. I'm older than most of the students, so I don't fraternize with them." He shrugged. "I'm there for an education."

"What will you do when you finish?"

Losing Caroline had made going to classes and working at the campground difficult because he had no goal except to graduate and survive, but he fought hard each day with an ache as big as one of these mountains and prayed someday he would find direction. He stopped walking. "That's a good question. I have no idea, but I'm majoring in business and figure it will come in handy no matter what I do."

"I see. What do you enjoy? Do you like numbers, data analysis, that sort of thing." She sounded interested as though she would help him make a decision right here and now.

"I could go for accounting, anything with numbers, but I'll decide later." He motioned toward the rustic Sky High Campground office. "We're almost there." They resumed their trek. "What about you? I'd peg you as a people person."

Her jaw fell open. "You're right, but what gave it away?"

Nick chuckled. "Got that security guard surveillance thing going for me," he said as they walked up the steps.

Nick held the door for her then pulled a chair in front of his desk. "Make yourself at home. I'll brew a pot of coffee."

Nick scooped the grounds into the coffee maker, added water, and started their pick me up. "I keep a roll of paper towels to use as napkins." He touched the holder at the end of the refreshment table. "Get yourself one."

The coffee gurgled.

"It's not gourmet, but help yourself."

~

Emily didn't care what it tasted like, it would warm her, and the cup would give her something to hold on to while she discussed the trespasser. She poured herself a drink, peeled off a faux napkin then turned around. "How about you?"

He lifted his left shoulder slightly. "Why not?"

She filled another cup and set the treats on the desk. As she took a seat across from him, he picked up the landline and punched in numbers. In moments he told the party on the other end what had happened at her cabin. "So, we wanted to see if you've had any crime over there."

Emily clicked her fingernails on the cup.

Silence then Nick hung up.

Emily leaned so far across the desk she was nearly on the other side of it. "Yes?"

"Not much going on, some shoplifting, a domestic dispute, that sort of thing."

"We already found something here." Emily pounded her fist on the desk.

Nick flinched. "We have a hole in the ground outside your cabin. That's it."

"Yes, but I heard the noise and saw the body. Someone was digging a grave in my yard."

Starting to think she would never convince Nick of the danger confronting her, she whispered when she said *digging a grave in my yard.* How many times did she have to tell him for him to believe her?

"I don't want you to worry."

Ha! If he acknowledged her plight, it would ease her anxiety. He'd know why she had the angst too.

He sat back in his chair and folded his arms over his chest. "I will handle this."

Emily called on all the restraint she had. Someone traipsed around her cabin with a corpse. She had no idea who, or why. It was obvious Nick didn't believe her. What did he intend to do? "I hope you can."

He stared at her as though he tried to see through her. "You do realize the ditch we saw wasn't as deep as we dig them here for a human." He uncrossed his arms. "I don't mean to come right out and say you're wrong, but people around here make their graves six feet deep to keep the animals from digging them up, even though most places go down only four since they started putting concrete boxes around the caskets."

Images of the man carrying the dead body flashed in Emily's mind. The blood drained from her head. The room started to spin. She grabbed the side of her chair.

"Ma'am, I didn't mean to upset you with talk of corpses, but you've said twice the hole in your yard is a grave. It isn't. I figured you didn't know much about graves in this area."

Nick squirmed in his seat as though it had ants in it.

"Miss Hanover, I'll make sure you're not harmed. Even though we don't know there's unlawful activity, I won't take any chances."

Finally, they were getting somewhere. Emily let a bit of optimism for help settle over her. "That's good. What will you do to protect us?" Maybe including him in her question would get him more involved in catching the trespasser.

"I'll come by your cabin throughout the night. Count on it." He touched his forefinger to his chest. "If you hear someone outside, it's me. However, if you see or hear suspicious activity and I'm not around, call my cell immediately. I will not be far away."

Emily flopped back in her chair.

"Please, don't let the noise or the trench in your yard upset you. I'll keep you safe."

Her insides raced every time she heard a loud clank. It didn't matter whether or not it sounded like someone hit rock. The racket signaled danger and made her jump. Right now, the ache in her head told her she was fighting a migraine, probably set off by Nick's continued doubt of her report about a serious crime. She could only try to trust his word. She'd know tonight if it was good.

"I'm fine." She swallowed hard. "I planned to refill my gas tank when I picked up groceries, but the station was running low. I checked again. Instead of getting more, they ran out. I have almost a quarter of a tank, but I can't get home on that. I'm stuck here, at least for a while."

"As I said, I will…"

What was he saying? Probably, he would keep her out of harm's way. She'd heard he would. Now she wanted to see him do it.

Chapter Three

Emily stood at the kitchen counter and brewed a pot of her herbal coffee, which aided digestion. She needed that tonight. After listening to Nick, she wished animals had turned over her trashcans and a hunter had carried a deer. Hmmp. That was no deer. At least Nick was right to pursue accounting instead of culinary arts. Saying his coffee wasn't gourmet put it mildly. She blew out a loud "Pfff." It probably wasn't his concoction that irritated her gastric system. More than likely, it was the entire situation.

Twilight cast its shadows across the landscape as she paced back and forth in front of the wall to wall sliding glass door, straining to see any activity while she waited for the coffee. Finally, the gurgling stopped. She poured a cup, sat down with it in the easy chair and sipped.

More than likely if she waited until later to eat, she'd be hungry enough to get food down. At ten o'clock she fixed a pimento cheese sandwich. After taking one bite, she grew nauseated and tossed her dinner in the trashcan. She liked pimento cheese and often packed a sandwich to take to work. Work.

Facing danger, she'd almost forgotten about her job.

Mostly, she reported on crimes after the fact. She did carry a Bible with her to offer to a criminal if she interviewed one. She intended to return to "Blue Mountain News" refreshed and ready to pick up where she left off. The only thing, Donnie was there.

Of course, God knew best. Someday she'd understand why she and Donnie shouldn't be together. Thoughts of his abandonment filled her with sadness, not to mention the anger churning in her like water about to boil. There was something about her Donnie didn't know though. Her strength came from God. Once she tapped into it, Donnie would be no more than a tiny ant on her path.

"I'm not doing this. I came to Sky High to relax. I'm going to read in the book I brought then get a good night's sleep."

She finally fell asleep at midnight.

At five o'clock loud crashing woke her. It sounded like a pan slipped off of the counter rattling as it hit the floor in the kitchen. She sprang up and pulled the covers around her.

Another pot fell. She scrunched into a tiny ball, pulling up the comforter. Maybe it was one of the indigents. Perhaps he would take some of her cereal and go away. What if he didn't leave? She scanned the room lit only by moonlight shining underneath the blinds. The footfalls grew louder, closer.

She got up, charged in the bathroom, and locked the door. No wait. He might break it down. With her chest constricting she darted to the bedroom, raised the blinds, crawled out the window, and shut it as the intruder switched on the inside light. She fell face down on the dirt, every muscle twitching.

Gradually, she squeezed her body against the outside wall. Inside, dresser drawers hit the floor. She flinched. Another thump. Another flinch. Then another. Finally, the world fell silent.

She was so cold. Frigid air blew around the corner of the cabin. If only she could go inside. She rose up and peeped in the window. A man with long hair with his back to her folded her clothes and returned them to the dresser drawers. She whimpered, placing her hand over her mouth to muffle the sound. Why was he putting everything away? She couldn't keep tears from rolling down her cheeks, and the shaking. She couldn't stop it.

She waited then looked inside again. The man was gone. She crawled indoors, shut the window, and locked it. Still shivering from fear and the frigid temperature, she crept down the hall touching the walls in the dark and continued to the kitchen / living area, where the light of the moon and stars filtered inside from the kitchen window. After her vision adjusted, she scanned the yard. He was no longer outside. Inside it looked as though he'd never been here.

Still, she wouldn't risk turning on a light in the living area or bedroom because he might linger in the woods watching the cabin. She made her way to the bathroom, which had a window with a dark shade, and switched on the overhead bulb. In the shower she let warm water run over her for thirty minutes until the cold from the night air disappeared. The icy chill she got because of the man who carried a body would remain with her until Nick caught him.

She trod into the bedroom and checked her watch—seven o'clock. Nick would be in the office at eight and so would she. The question was, if he were patrolling last night, how did he not see her intruder?

She forced down a piece of toast for breakfast and dressed in a pair of jeans and a T-shirt. With each step she took toward the manager's office, her blood pressure went up for wanting to know where Nick was while she was crouched outside her window.

Maybe he strolled around the front of the structure. Maybe that was why the man left. A squirrel sat on his hind legs on a fallen tree branch, his paws holding a nut to his mouth, his little jaws working. As she passed by, he flipped his tail and scurried away. She didn't mean to frighten the cute, little creature. She knew how he felt.

When she entered the office, Nick stood at his desk, whistling as he arranged papers. He looked up and his happy tune dwindled to nothing.

"How may I help you?"

So far Nick's performance had disappointed and aggravated her. Taking a deep breath, she called on every ounce of composure she had. After all, her world at Sky High consisted of her, Nick, and the man carrying the body, whoever he was. "I assume you looked around the cabin several times last night as you said you would."

Nick grasped the edge of the desk. "Yes, I most certainly did. Everything was fine."

"It wasn't fine? Someone entered my cabin, threw pots and pans on the floor in the kitchen and emptied the drawers in the bedroom."

Nick plopped down in his chair, his expression as startled as if someone had hit him. "Uh, that's, that's, not possible. Every time I walked around the structure, there was no one out there but me and a possum." He ran his hand through his hair. "I can't believe this. Are you sure?"

Emily sent him a harsh stare.

"Okay. I'm sorry, but at least you aren't harmed."

No thanks to him.

"I'll investigate the premises. Did you touch anything?"

Cooperation at last. A soldier as well as a security guard, he could handle the problem, if he set his mind to it. "Uh, no, I didn't have to. He took care of that for me, returning the clothes he'd taken out of the chest of drawers. He wore gloves though."

"He what?"

Emily nodded. "I'm telling you this has nothing to do with animals. It's weird. I guess that's why you won't believe he was there."

"No, I mean, yes, I do believe you. I'll examine the place for clues."

"Like what?"

Nick tilted his head. "Was any food missing?"

Nick did have ideas and strategies that never occurred to her. If only he put them to use. "I don't know. I didn't check the cabinets or the fridge."

"We'll see. Sometimes we have nesters, the forest people in the woods who come into what they believe are vacant homes looking for a place to live for the winter, or at least get leftovers for a meal. I hate doing it, but of course, I have to run them out of the cabins. Sometimes I leave sandwiches on the office steps. They all disappear. Generally, the folks we see up here can't cope with society the way we've set it up, or they're vets who can't adjust after serving. They're harmless."

If that were true, she wasn't buying the forest person scenario about the man who was digging in her yard. And Nick left sandwiches for indigents? He was a complicated person. "I understand, but why would a homeless person dig a ditch and rummage through my kitchen cabinets and clothes without taking anything?"

"Some of the unfortunate are veterans who left the war with brain injuries or PTSD. Maybe he thought he was burying a dead soldier when he dug the hole." Nick divided a pile of papers on his desk and put them down. "Perhaps, he needed clothing."

Emily took Nick's words to heart. Yet, in the final analysis, she wanted to rest and recover from her own recent trauma, which she had to admit, paled in comparison to the scenario he described.

Nick stood and motioned toward the door. "Let's see what we have." Touching her gently, he placed his hand on her back to guide her outdoors. This time she detected a sensitivity she'd never experienced with Donnie. She couldn't dwell on that now though. He walked fast, and she had to keep up. They arrived at the cabin within ten minutes.

After they went inside Emily searched the kitchen. "I'm not missing any food."

Nick squatted down and studied a spot on the floor. "There's a bit of dirt here, but I don't see a shoe pattern." He stood. "You say he was in the bedroom?"

"Yes. Follow me." Emily led the way and on Nick's request, she checked the drawers and closet. "I'm not missing anything in here either." She started toward the bathroom. "I know all of my items are still in there because I took a shower earlier."

Nick clasped his arms behind his body. "All right. If

you don't mind, I'll take a look around."

So far, his theory, which was starting to rub her nerves like sandpaper, had gotten them nowhere. "Mind? Absolutely not. It would delight me if we solved this problem. I could get on with my vacation."

Nick wandered about, stopping to stare at the floor, walls, and furniture. "I don't see much." He pointed to the floor. "Some of the impressions on the carpet are heavier than others, but that tells me very little. Possibly one day you trod with a heavy foot, or someone who weighs more than you walked on it."

Emily put her hand over her mouth. "I heard him stomping in the kitchen."

"Uh-huh. Maybe he was looking for something and grew angry when he didn't find it."

"What? What could he have been looking for?"

Nick shook his head. "I haven't a clue. As I said, around here intruders are usually those who need food, but if none's missing…" Nick's voice trailed. "I'll keep better watch over you. I'm not convinced there's anyone harmful up here, but I have to admit, between the hole and the break-in, I'm suspicious."

Suspicious? He must be awfully hard headed. What would it take to convince him?

He bit his bottom lip. "Did you leave the door unlocked?"

What? Did he think she was an idiot? She bit her tongue to keep words as sharp as barbed wire from flying from it. "Of course not. I heard a thump when he went out. As to how he got in, I'm clueless."

Nick squared his stance. "The windows stay secure unless a guest opens them?"

Emily snapped him a look. "Really? You think I'd

leave one open after I saw a man carrying around a dead body?"

Nick lowered his gaze. "Sorry, no. Hmm. I suppose it's possible the cleaning crew did." He examined the casements in the bedroom and bathroom. "I imagine you would've heard him if he'd broken in. Still, I'll inspect all of the locks."

"Thank you."

"Sure."

Progress.

Nick pulled back the sliding glass door spanning the wall in the living area without unfastening it.

Emily gasped. "No," she whispered. Then she gathered herself. "The cleaning crew, huh?"

"Uh, uh, of course, not." He directed his attention to the door. "Uu-uh, this old lock has a build-up of dirt. I'll install a new one today." Nick looked like a puppy that knew it had offended its owner. He took a picture of the malfunctioning device and glanced at Emily. "See if there's a ruler or tape measure in one of the cabinet drawers."

Emily rushed into the kitchen, snatched a ruler, and hurried back. As far as she was concerned, he couldn't secure the latch quick enough.

He measured it, took a few notes, and flew out, the front door banging behind him.

She had to sit down. It was one thing to hear noises and think someone made them, but to have proof knocked her off of her feet. Who had been in the cabin and why?

Chapter Four

Late in the afternoon Emily went to the front porch and sat in a rocking chair. She pushed her feet on the floor and rocked as the sun set on the mountains in brilliant colors of red and orange. The day waned ever so slowly as though it wanted one last breath before twilight.

She should embrace this beautiful evening. The quiet should soothe her soul, but each time a twig broke she stiffened until no one appeared or she saw a squirrel. Scooting to the edge of the rocker, she listened for the next snap. She had thought God called her to this place of tranquility to wrap His arms around her, bring her comfort, and refresh her spirit. He would not have called her to this. She no longer knew why she came, but these hills pulled at her as though they would not let her go until she found out.

As she stood and stretched her stomach growled. She went to the kitchen, snatched two pieces of bread, and the pimento cheese. Odd, how the situation had seemed under control in the daylight when Nick reassured her. She spread the cheese on the bread in frantic strokes. Now, every muscle in her body tightened. Twilight turned to night. Evil could hide in the darkness and pounce at any moment.

She got a cup of coffee, sat at the kitchen table, bit into her dinner, and forced down a small bite despite the fact she loved pimento cheese. Where was Nick? He'd said he would bring a new lock for the sliding glass door.

She managed to get down the rest of her food—barely. As she picked up her plate and mug, someone knocked on her door. She set the dishes on the counter then peered out the window and saw her guest. She swung the door open. "Come in."

Nick held up a bag from Broken Arrow Hardware. "I hope I'm not interrupting your evening. I have the lock."

"Definitely not." She couldn't remember a time when she welcomed an intrusion more. "I'm grateful you brought it."

"You bet. It shouldn't take too long to replace the old one."

Intense concentration took over Nick's countenance as he unwrapped the lock and read the instructions. Not wanting to distract him when he squatted down and went to work, Emily sat on the sofa. She tried to read in a book, but she peeked every couple of pages to check on Nick's progress. After an hour he stood and brushed off his hands.

"There you go. No one will get in here tonight. You're locked up tighter than Fort Knox."

"Thank you."

Nick packed his small toolbox. "Have a nice evening. Don't worry. I'll walk around the outside of the cabin throughout the night."

"Sounds good." Emily secured the front door behind him.

Rather than help put the hurtful events of her wedding day behind her, so far this vacation had added more stress. Surely, Nick would catch whoever lurked outside then broke in. The sooner she could get on with her plan for renewal the better. Other than reading, which had eluded her so far, it included hiking, watching the animals, and relishing the sunsets. She stretched out on the sofa, laid back on a pillow, and let sleep overtake her until she heard knocking.

She sprang up and tip-toed to the door, peering through the peephole. "Thank goodness." She opened it. "Come in."

Nick stepped just inside the entryway. "I wanted to let you know everything looks fine. As I said, you have nothing to worry about. Get a good night's rest."

"Thank you. I'm glad you stopped by to tell me you're out there. I'm sure I'll sleep better."

Nick nodded. "Good Miss Hanover, enjoy the rest of your evening."

"Emily. Please call me Emily."

"Yes, ma'am, uh, Emily. You can call me Nick."

"Okay, Nick." Emily shut the door then locked and bolted it. Oh, how she wished Nick had stayed a little while. Having someone near who cared about her safety would have calmed her, made her isolation less frightening. Should she have invited him inside for coffee? Or would a visit have gone beyond his job description?

Unable to sit still, she paced around the room, turned out the lights in the kitchen and drew the curtains. If last night's intruder were outside the cabin earlier and saw them open, he realized someone inside closed them. A chill fell over her and she rubbed her arms.

It appeared the man who went through her kitchen and bedroom drawers failed to find what he wanted. Tonight, she wouldn't sleep a wink. She grabbed her e-reader from the sofa and turned out all of the lights. She could still see the words on the lighted page. A good book would take her mind off of everything.

Not that she wanted homelessness for anyone, but since Nick had mentioned it, she wished she could believe the man she saw was a pitiful indigent simply looking for dinner. Actually, if she did, she'd leave food for him, but this was far more nefarious.

She situated herself in the hall on the floor in the event the e-reader emitted more light than she thought. For the next two hours she read only a few pages. She had no idea what this novel was about. She kept starting over because the noises she'd heard her first night here banged around in her mind. She put her hands over her ears. Please, not again tonight.

She dozed until twelve-thirty when a noise woke her. Maybe it was Nick. He'd said if she heard someone outdoors, it was him, but she didn't see his flashlight and suddenly the same scraping and hitting she'd heard on Thursday night wafted inside. It sounded farther away this time, but it was out there.

She dropped the e-reader and paced up and down the hall, her skin tingling as if spiders crawled over it. Finally, she charged into the bedroom, pulled her cell out of her purse, and called Nick. He didn't answer. She waited a few minutes and tried again. She sent a text.

No response. Why didn't he answer? Had the killer attacked him? She fanned herself, wandered into the living area, and sat on the sofa. She could try Nick later. What if he didn't reply on purpose because he was the one digging? Could she trust him? After all, she didn't really know him.

More racket resounded. With or without Nick she'd get to the bottom of this racket. When Larry checked her into Sky High, he had given her the number for the sheriff's office at Broken Arrow, but she needed to have a good reason to call. Not an animal digging or a big empty hole. She couldn't even credibly claim someone had been in the cabin since nothing was stolen.

She took deep breaths. She could no longer wait for someone to attack her, she had to do something. She'd find out who was out there and get evidence to give to the sheriff, but first she had to calm down and make a plan. She put her phone in her coat pocket as well as pepper spray and the flashlight from the kitchen. Pointing the flashlight down she cupped her hand over it and walked onto the porch into the shadows. The night was overcast, so she could hide without much trouble. An award-winning division one collegiate runner, if someone did come after her, she could outrun them.

~

Nick rubbed his hand through his hair. Just his luck, these suspicious incidents at Emily's cabin occurred now, right after he took semester finals. He was beyond tired. He finished his walk around the cabin. Everything seemed fine. There were no lights on inside. She'd probably gone to sleep. Lucky her.

It was twelve forty-five when he returned to the manager's quarters at the office. To keep awake, he consumed an entire pot of coffee, and he was still sleepy. Surely, he could set his phone and take a one-hour nap. He couldn't explain why someone dug the suspicious-looking hole. Nothing he'd seen suggested a crime. His mind filled with potential explanations. Perhaps the owner tilled the yard for a flower bed that wasn't finished yet. An elk still sporting antlers could easily have sharpened them on the boulders and created a scraping noise.

Whatever, if he didn't at least nap, he was going to fall asleep before he could make another round. He set his alarm for one-forty-five, leaned over his desk, crossed his arms, and rested his head on them, zonking out.

He slept peacefully until a clunk jarred him. Surveying the area, he noticed his business accounting book on the floor. He must've knocked it off in his sleep. The profits and loss statements section he wanted to review before he started next semester would have to wait. He yawned. Then he picked up his cell. "Nooo." He'd slept through the alarm and the phone ringing. Emily had called three times. He sprang from his seat and charged to the cabin.

Chapter Five

At one o'clock Emily stepped off of the porch into the dark, her footfalls echoing into the wind, her hands shaking the flashlight's beam into flickers. She'd told herself many times a little apprehension would keep her alert. Counting on her theory, she shinned the light in front of her then to the right and the left. Nothing.

Loud clanking rang into the night. Her insides quivered. She was grounded in reality no matter what Nick thought. She did not hear or see things that weren't there, or mistake animals for people. There it was again.

As she walked toward it, she trembled, but like Tarzan with a flashlight, she pounded her free fist against her chest. She would confront man or beast with sticks, rocks, pepper spray, whatever it took. She travelled here to rest, pray in this awe-inspiring part of the world and leave refreshed, ready to start a new life. She intended to carry out her plan. Her future depended on finding and recapturing the Emily she knew before Donnie buried her psyche.

The naked forest fell quiet, except for the sound of sticks breaking in the distance. Even though her insides twisted into knots, she kept walking into the damp, cold, air, winding her way between the shadows of gray, leafless trees and underbrush. A light shined back at her.

Her resolve deflated. She switched off her light and hid behind a large boulder. The blackness fell around her like a shroud while luminous beams danced on a figure moving toward her.

A cell phone rang. The figure turned around and answered. A silhouette in the glow of his light, he was so close to her she could see his medium build and long hair at the base of his neck. What color was his hair? And his features? She strained to see, but it was too dark.

"What do you want? Yes, I told you I'd get out here and get it done."

Silence.

"It's still the perfect place."

The perfect place for what? To bury the dead body? Emily shivered.

"I went to the campground yesterday. It was completely deserted except for the security guard. I saw him, but he didn't see me."

Silence.

"I thought I saw a light a few minutes ago, but it's gone now. I'm going to look around. If there's anyone out here, I'll take care of it."

Take care of it? How? Murder her? Emily froze. But she had to find out where he was to know where to hide. She braved a step forward to peek around the rock. A twig cracked underneath her feet. She squeezed her eyes shut and shook all over. Now, she had to move. Carefully, she tip-toed over the sticks into the shadow of an oak tree. He was so close she could see his misty breath. And his high forehead, wrinkled like a bulldog's. Another breaking branch echoed into the night. She lifted her foot off of it. It was too late. Footfalls came closer and closer as though he had her on radar. *Lord, please help me.*

He swung his flashlight toward the tree trunk and the earth beneath Emily spun. The man said, "Oh, it's you" as a black curtain dropped over her field of vision right before she passed out.

She woke up and saw an elk standing over her. How long had she been unconscious? Where'd the elk come from? She sat up then scooted against the tree trunk. Should she give thanks for the elk? Or fear him? Wait. She remembered. If an elk's too close, hide. Barely breathing, she waited. He must've thought she was part of the woods, and the man must've thought she was the elk. Talk about a blessing.

Minutes later the elk left. She rose a little at a time like the sun coming up, got on her feet, and leaned against the tree until she knew she could walk. Still a bit woozy, she stepped with caution while keeping the flashlight pointed down until she reached the cabin.

She approached the porch as though she walked on ice, looking carefully to her right and left. Once indoors after the key clicked, she passed the rustic walls of the kitchen, down the hall to the bedroom and fell on the bed. She looked at her watch—four o'clock. She'd been in the frigid temperature for three hours. Thank goodness, she had worn plenty of warm clothes plus her down coat. She switched off the flashlight and left off the lamp. Best not to have on any light.

What she wouldn't give for a hot shower. Instead,

she lay wide awake peering into the darkness, waiting for the evil lurking outside to enter. Where was Nick?

~

Panting, Nick ran to Emily's cabin. Gravel flew up from his boots all the way. Still, there were no lights. All appeared well. He bent over, put his palms on his knees and caught his breath. Why did she call him? Should he call her? No, he couldn't wake her up at two o'clock in the morning. What if something awful happened? He cared more than he should, and he wasn't sure why.

Taking care of the guests at Sky High Campground was his job. Where should he look for her? She probably wasn't in eminent danger, but upset? You bet, or she wouldn't have called. It tore him up inside. He walked onto the porch. He did have a universal key. Should he use it? He paced back and forth. He focused on the door. In moments he snatched the key from his pocket.

Be quiet. Move at a slow, steady pace. Don't stomp, or make any noise that might wake her. Just see if she's alright. Nick shined his flashlight around the kitchen and sitting area. She wasn't here. Of course not. She wouldn't stay awake in the dark until all hours of the morning. He clicked his tongue. He hated to invade her privacy. He'd take a quick look into the bedroom, see if she was asleep. Stepping lightly, he peeked inside the room. She wasn't here.

"Nooo." He dropped the flashlight and put his face in his hands. "No. No. No." What a fool he'd been. He had to find her before it was too late. Was it too late already? His pulse beat in his temples.

He yanked up the flashlight, locked the door and ran

out of the house. *Calm down. Use your head.* Where would she go? He stopped and listened. For what? Anything that would tell him where she was. Had someone kidnapped her? *Oh, please Lord, let her be alright. Not only because of my job, but…Oh please, Lord.*

Something had drawn him to Emily. Compassion? Partly, but it was more. She was so attractive. It was chemistry. No, she wasn't attractive. She was beautiful with haunting hazel eyes with long lashes. Her dainty nose. Flowing auburn hair. He'd seen beautiful women since Caroline, and when he did, he only thought of Caroline. When he looked at Emily, all he saw was Emily. He didn't know why, but with every ounce of desire in him, he wanted to know her better. He couldn't lose her now to a monster in a cold, dark forest.

He stood like a statue in the quiet waiting for metal to scrape rock, but he didn't hear a sound. An image of Emily fighting flashed in his mind. Yes, she would fight, to escape. He closed his eyelids. Not from guilt this time. He could not face losing her. Where could she be? The peace of the forest, quiet except for a few broken twigs and the wind blowing, held no signals of danger or evil.

He heard footsteps and jerked to his right. An elk took long strides with his slender legs. He needed a clue, not to see an elk. Poor thing probably only wanted food. It stopped and stretched its thick neck upward, looking regal, but then ran away as though it sensed a threat. Did the elk hear the noise he could not?

He pivoted and charged to the area where the elk had been. *Clank, clank, clank.* It was faint, but audible.

His only lead. He sped toward the clatter. It grew louder. Panting, he ran faster and faster. Nothing, not even a mountain lion, could keep him from finding the clanks.

Clank, clank, clank.

Surveying the area, he started to sweat in the frigid night air. He should've taken Emily's complaints more seriously. Charging forward, he followed the clanking. It sounded as though it was right beside him.

All of a sudden, it stopped.

His back clicked into a rod. He stood still, listening to the silence pounding in his brain. He would not leave until he found Emily. He charged the area like a bull. She had to be here. With every muscle pulled as tight as a violin string he stared into the dark, running into the unknown until he slid into a hole. He tingled all over. A hole just like the one in Emily's front yard. He gasped. There was another one. He put his hands on the side of the ditch and pulled himself onto level ground. No sign of Emily. How evil was the person creating the noise?

Chapter Six

Exhausted, Emily slept until two o'clock in the afternoon. Of course, she missed the morning sunrise, the pancakes she had intended to make for breakfast, and the long hike she had planned to take at Sky High when she decided to come here. She did rest for the first time since she'd arrived, and she needed that. She charged her cell phone again and called the gas station. No luck getting fuel.

She had to convince Nick someone carried a dead body across her yard. Then, maybe he would make an effort to catch the trespasser. Knowing no one else believed a murderer ran free at Sky High sent a quiver through her bones. Enough.

She sat up in bed and ran her hand through her hair. She intended to give that good-looking security guard a piece of her mind this afternoon when she let him know she saw someone in the woods. He had said he would check on her. Ha! She was in this on her own. He was about as much help as a fly at a dinner party. He must've gotten through life thus far on his good looks.

She showered, put on her fancy jeans with the flowers embroidered on one leg and the hot pink sweater that matched the embroidery. She'd brought them on the off chance she might have something special to attend, and of course, a dress too. What was she thinking?

She had known it wouldn't be like the spring or summer, but while she had been too upset to think about the winter slow months when packing, she'd never dreamed the only people here would be her, a criminal, and a security guard.

At a minimum, she hoped Nick would at least acknowledge someone trespassed. Maybe then she could unwind and clear her mind in the tranquil environment she sought when she arrived. At least she loved this place, all of the wonderful memories, the peace it usually offered, and the views, magnificent and awe-inspiring even this time of the year.

She took a little extra care of her hair and put on powder and mascara before she left. She didn't know why, probably to brighten the darkness in her life. The white, puffy clouds had turned to gray while the wind had grown bitter. She doubted she'd get caught in the rain on the short walk, but if she did, she'd drink some of Nick's awful coffee and warm up.

A disheveled, dirty-looking figure emerged from the woods as she rounded a curve and started toward the office. She darted behind a large trash can, her heart racing. No one else was supposed to be on the property. The man digging holes and slamming rock in her yard. Who else could it be? She put her hand over her mouth to hold in a gasp. He turned left then right. His coat flew open. A gun at his belt.

She wrapped her arms around her chest to stop shaking. Where was Nick? If he could see the man with the weapon, he'd believe her. He'd know the man had been carrying around someone he killed. She was okay though. Only a deranged person would attack someone in broad daylight. Maybe he was deranged. She pulled up her knees and held them to her chest trying to make herself small.

He was on the street. She had to stop trembling. She was going to rattle the trashcan. Why didn't he go away, crawl back in his hole? His steps turned up gravel. Was he headed toward her?

The crunching stopped. Maybe Nick was in his office. Maybe he spotted the man through the window. Captured him. Her spirits sank. Did Nick ever do anything, or did he just sit around and drink that stuff he called coffee? Footsteps closer. Shaking all over, she looked up.

Wide-eyed, Nick peered at her. Pine needles stuck out from his bangs, the only deviation from his military haircut. Dirt covered his gray pants, his shirt torn. Had he run into a cougar?

He crossed his arms over his chest. "What are you doing behind the trash can? How long have you been there?"

Who did he think he was talking to her in a harsh tone of voice? "Where have you been?" It dawned on her. He was here now, and she was safe. She let out a sigh of relief as her muscles relaxed and she slumped into a heap.

He pulled her up in one swoop and hugged her.

His strength wrapped around her like a cocoon.

He released his grip, then stepped back. "Thank God, you're here."

"Yeah, I've been thanking Him every morning after surviving another night." The frightening moments, more intense each time, chipped at her independence. She wanted to stay at Sky High. She could resolve the anger and disappointment her failed wedding caused in this tranquil, beautiful place. Yet, she couldn't confront this criminal alone. In spite of the yearning to remain nagging her in the back of her head, she'd be better off to leave. "What do you hear about the gas situation. I'm ready to pack…"

He laid his hand on her arm, his touch so gentle it calmed her.

"Shhh. No," he said, his tone as soft as his touch. He guided her toward the manager's office. "I'm going to contact, Larry, the main security guard, tell him what's going on, and let him know, not ask, let him know, I'm moving into the cabin next to yours."

His words confused Emily. Did he finally believe her? "Oh."

"Come in, and I'll make us some coffee."

Emily offered him a faint smile. "Why don't I make it? You might want to freshen up." She preferred her brew, and she imagined he did want to change.

He peered at his pants and shirt. "Uh, yes. Actually, if it's not too much trouble, I'll take you up on your offer."

"Sure." At last, something went her way.

They went inside and Nick left. Soon the sound of water running wafted into the office. By the time she'd fixed their drinks, he appeared in a pair of jeans and a brown checked shirt. The color set off his dark eyes and long lashes, so much so it seemed he looked right through her, reading her thoughts. She saw his fine features, a straight nose and high cheek bones in a different light, not just a good-looking guy, but a man who appealed to her. Heat built inside her and rushed to her cheeks.

"Hmm, that smells good, and I sure could use it."

Good. He was focused on the coffee, not the spell he'd cast over her. "Uh." She set the cups and two paper towels on his desk. "Where have you been?"

He sat down in his desk chair then she took a seat across from him.

He sipped his drink. "Looking for you." He said the words as though she should have known the answer before she asked.

Relief washed over Emily. He cared about her safety. "I'm puzzled. I thought you were going to come by the cabin during the night?"

Nick put down his cup. "I intended to. I mean I did. I …let me explain. First, don't think you can't count on me. You can. It won't happen again."

Emily rubbed the back of her neck. Yeah, at some point it might occur to him that she could report his negligence to Larry—in spite of the allure of his eyes. "What won't happen again? As far as I can tell you haven't done anything." Emily sighed. "Period."

Nick blew out a loud breath. "That's what I'm trying to tell you. From now on I'm going to watch you like a hawk."

Emily leaned forward. "Why? Something's going on, right? What changed your mind?"

"The holes."

"Holes, what holes?"

"The ones in the woods."

"There are holes in the woods?" Emily blinked. "I heard the metal striking stone, but I didn't see a hole. I guess it was too dark."

"You didn't see a hole? When?" He wrung his hands. "You were in the woods?"

"Yes, somebody has to get to the bottom of this, and I haven't seen anyone else trying to solve the problem. Last night I couldn't sleep for wanting to find proof this guy's destroying property, at best. Since a video is worth a thousand words, I decided to capture him in action. You weren't convinced after you saw the trench in my yard." Emily clenched her jaw tight. "I guess those in the forest are different."

Nick cocked an eyebrow. "No, they looked exactly like the one in your yard. I'm sorry it had to come to this for me to listen to you." He looked away as though he couldn't face her then returned his gaze. "We do have forest people come and go in the winter. Sometimes they do strange things." He sent Emily a tight-lipped smile. "I went to your cabin last night. You weren't there."

"I left at one o' clock in the morning. My plan wasn't to haul someone into custody, but to gather evidence. I'm not crazy. There is something really strange going on at Sky High. I don't intend to be collateral damage."

Nick pulled at his shirt collar. "I hear you. I came by at nine o'clock, eleven o'clock, and planned to return every hour after that. I missed so much sleep studying for my finals before I arrived here only to miss more sleep over this situation. I laid my head on the desk to rest for a little bit. The next thing I knew, I woke up at two o'clock. I rushed to the cabin, but you were gone. I haven't been to sleep since. I spent the entire night looking for you." Nick pointed his finger toward her. "Look, I don't know what all of these holes mean, but as I said, I'm moving right next door to you."

The poor guy was as exhausted as she was. She'd only thought of herself. She wanted to crawl under her chair.

He sipped his drink. "Hey, this is delicious. It doesn't taste like mine. Did you use a different bag?"

Emily loved coffee. She prided herself on finding her delicious herbal flavor. Knowing she concocted something special with Nick's blend added to her satisfaction. "No. I'm glad you like it though. Would you like more?"

He held his cup in midair and looked at it. "Not right now, but I'm sure I'll have some later to get through the day."

"Good. After all the sleep you lost, you're going to need it. I have an idea though."

"What?"

"For now, why don't you take a nap?"

He sat straight up. "Beg your pardon."

"I know you're not supposed to sleep at work, but you're not supposed to stay up all night either. Trust me. I'll call around six to wake you. I could make some coffee better than this." Emily tapped her cup, giving herself time to conjure up a bit more courage for what she was about to say. "Then you can come to the cabin. I'll treat you to coffee and pancakes."

He smiled like a kid someone offered an ice cream cone. "Is this an invitation? I thought you hated me."

Emily twisted her paper towel. "Well, I, uh. I was thinking…"

He got up and hit the desk with his palm. "Don't answer that. Sounds like an excellent plan."

Emily stood. "Good. I'll call you at six."

Nick took hold of the back of his desk chair and leaned forward. "Be careful. Text me when you get to the cabin, please."

"Will do." Knowing Nick cared whether or not she arrived home safely gave her comfort. She walked out with the first inkling of contentment she'd gotten since the defunct wedding. The sky didn't look quite as gray. *Hmm.* Nick had spent all night searching for her. Of course, he was a person who took his duty seriously, someone she was glad to finally have on her side. Since he now believed she dealt with a credible threat, he probably would stay on high alert and not rest until he caught the culprit. How long would that take?

Chapter Seven

Emily entered the cabin. For the first time since she heard the noise outside, the coziness of the sitting area wrapped around her. Her surroundings seemed more like a home away from home. She picked up her eReader and relaxed in the easy chair.

At six o'clock she called Nick. "It's your wake-up call."

He moaned then silence fell. "Uh, yeah. I'll see you at seven."

She hung up the phone with a sense of peace washing over her like soft rain. Having pancakes with Nick was at least a small consolation if she couldn't leave the campground. Perhaps she had disliked him at first because of her angst toward Donnie. Even though she hadn't meant to, she suspected she had.

Well, Nick doubting her when she told him about the strange activity in her yard created resentment, but she had to admit she could see his side of the situation. No one had reported anyone dead or missing. There wasn't a body at the campground and the authorities in Blue Mountain and Broken Arrow mentioned only petty crimes. She sighed. Alas. He believed her now though. The creep who banged around her yard then entered her cabin was about to get caught—she hoped.

She could understand why Nick attributed the hole in her yard to a disturbed veteran. Yet, Nick didn't mention the intruder going through the drawers in her bedroom. Was a disturbed vet looking for clothing? She drummed her fingers on the arm of the chair. Thoughts turned in her mind like a kaleidoscope. The break-in didn't make sense. Would Nick start putting the pieces together since he had decided to look into the incidents? She glanced at her watch. Seven o'clock.

A series of knocks landed on her door right on time.

Nick flashed a toothpaste ad smile and handed her a bud vase with three red roses.

She let out a soft gasp as warmth covered her like sunshine. "Ah. Thank you."

"I went to the General Store and found these. Since you're stuck in less-than-ideal circumstances on Valentine's Day…" he cleared his throat…"that's an understatement. Anyway, I thought you should have something special."

"That's so considerate. They're lovely." She floated to the small kitchen table and set the flowers on it, standing back to admire them. "They're the perfect finishing touch."

Valentine's Day. After all that had happened, she'd forgotten about the holiday. She hoped he didn't pity her because she told him about Donnie. That was the last thing she needed, but nonetheless, the roses were a sweet gesture, especially for someone so unemotional.

"Can I do something?"

Emily scanned the kitchen. "Yes. If you like, get out the butter and syrup while I cook the pancakes. I wanted to serve them hot, so I waited until now to start cooking them.”

“Sure.” Nick walked to the refrigerator and then the cabinet as though he knew his way around the place.

Soon little bubbles appeared on the batter in the pan. Emily flipped the pancakes and cooked the other side before she placed them on their plates with sausage links.

Nick pivoted. “I see the cups. We’re having coffee, right?”

“Yes.”

“I’ll pour our drinks.”

In moments they sat down amid the sweet aromas of hazelnut and syrup. Nick glanced at his plate then directed his attention to Emily. “I’ll say grace if that’s okay.”

“Absolutely.”

They bowed their heads and Nick blessed their meal.

After he took a bite, his countenance lit up as bright as a kid’s on Christmas morning. “Delicious. It’s been a long time since I ate a home-cooked meal. I’ll tell you, field rations, college cafeteria food, and my eggs and coffee don’t measure up to this.”

Emily chuckled. “I’m glad you’re enjoying it.” For the first time since Thursday night, she didn’t have to force her food down her throat.

Nick sipped his drink. “Ahh, yes! This is great.” He held up his cup. “What kind is it? I’m going to get some to keep at the office.”

Leave no doubt, he appeared to enjoy the meal. Emily wanted the same to go for her company. Until she heard that shovel hitting stone, she’d been so lost in pain, she didn’t know she needed a friend. If nothing else, the horror surrounding her vacation had awakened her desire to re-join the human race—with caution. "It's an herbal blend. I order it online if you'd like the URL, uh…" Wait. What an opportunity to get rid of the bitter tasting stuff he made. "I tell you what, I'll order some and gift it to the office."

"You don't need to do that."

"I want to. *Honestly*."

"Are you sure?"

"Definitely." Emily could hardly get the word out soon enough.

"Well, if you insist."

She would not take any chance he might forget to place the order. "You have so much to do. I'm not all that busy, except when I'm trying to catch a murderer on my phone's camera."

Nick put his hand on hers and his touch ignited a sweet sensation. "You're not to go out alone again ever." He took the last bite of his dinner and gulped his drink. "I called Larry, told him what was happening, and let him know I intended to move out of the manager's quarters tonight."

Emily gulped the last of her drink and sat straight up. "Oh. Can I help with that?"

"No, I travel light—clothes, a few groceries, and personal items. It won't take long." Nick looked at his watch. "If we clean this up, I can move in and get settled by eleven o'clock. Thank goodness, the threat of rain has passed." He stood, pushed in his chair, and looked at her with eyes as soft as a whisper.

Sensing a longing, Emily met his gaze.

Finally, he glimpsed his plate then picked it up. "I'll gather these if you'll put them in the dishwasher."

"Uh, no. I mean, you don't need to do that. Go pack. I'll take care of these."

"All right. Next time I do the dishes?"

She had not given Nick enough credit. There was more to this ex-military / security guy than his good looks. If the way to a man's heart was through his stomach as the old saying went, the way to hers was through the dishwasher. Cooking alone inconvenienced her more than enough.

She jolted. He'd said, "Next time." Granted, his statement sounded more like a question. Was he asking if she'd like to see him again? In spite of the pain Donnie caused and the crazy noises, a light, airy sensation fell over her. She didn't much care what Donnie had done. She fiddled with a button on her blouse. "Sure. I'll take you up."

Nick's lips curled on the corners. "I better get going. In a few hours you'll have a next-door neighbor who leaves his lights on all night. If that doesn't discourage anyone who comes around uninvited, the trespasser will pay for his mistake." Nick walked to the door and started out then he looked over his shoulder. "Call if you need me. I turned up the volume on my phone. I'll hear it from now on even if I'm asleep."

"Okay."

Nick shut the door.

Emily started putting the plates in the dishwasher. This vacation was nothing like she'd planned, but it just took a turn for the better. If Nick could only catch the man banging around.

She couldn't stop thinking about the corpse, yearning to know where it was and how it was connected to her cabin. The crime reporter in her wouldn't let her stop trying to figure out the mystery. Most recently, as far as they knew, the trespasser had dug two holes in the woods. She sucked in a deep breath. Why? How many people did he want to bury? Or did he want to do something else? If so, what? She wanted to pull her hair out.

Thank goodness, Nick was nearby. Knowing someone else would hear the man digging and possibly capture him, relieved her anxiety. Convinced she could enjoy at least a bit of the tranquility she sought when she came here, she stretched to relax, the same as she did after she completed an important article. Then she curled up on the sofa and read until she dozed off.

A scraping noise woke her at midnight. She jumped straight up, but wait. Surely, Nick heard it too. She turned her ear toward the window, waiting for the encore. The man outside banged rock over and over this time as though he tried to beat it into pieces.

With her pulse racing she got up and peeped out the crack between the curtains on the sliding glass door. It was pitch-black outside. Where was Nick? And what about the lights he intended to leave on.

Maybe she should call him. She got out her cell phone as spotlights lit up the cabin next door like a parking lot, illumination streaming onto part of her yard. With his long hair flying, a man darted into the woods. Nick struck out after him. Emily walked onto her front porch, staring into the dark forest, biting her fingernail. The sound of feet pounded the ground like a stampede of elk. Itching to know what was happening, she walked closer to the edge of the trees and squinted to see.

She had escaped unscathed from the woods last

night. Nick would do the same, wouldn't he? She wrung her hands. If she and Nick knew what the creep had done with the body, they could get help from the authorities.

She focused on the cold, black forest until her insides twisted in fear for Nick. Shivering she realized she stood outside without her coat. The frigid air bit her cheek, but she would not move from here. Staring into the darkness that swallowed Nick, she waited. *Lord, please bring Nick out of that abyss safely.* When would he reappear in the light?

The ends of her fingers grew numb. She stuck them inside her palms as she peered at the scrawny trees. Like them, she could do nothing but stand here as though everything was fine while wickedness invaded the wee hours of the morning. The usual sounds of twigs and branches broke into the lonely silence.

Odd, she'd arrived at the campground aware of nothing but the shame and sorrow devouring her, and out of the blue, terror struck like lightning. Even if Nick's concern came from a sense of duty, knowing she wasn't alone gave her an ounce of well-being.

Generating heat, she shuffled her feet and wiggled around. Finally, footsteps. Hardly able to breathe, she sucked air in ragged gulps. A shadowy figure moved in the pale moonlight. Nick. Oh, please, let it be Nick. Sticks cracked one right after the other. Staccato snaps pierced the quiet. The cracking grew louder. Emily's lips trembled as she waited—for Nick? An attack?

A male figure zig-zagged like he'd lost his way. She leaned forward. No hair flew on the silhouette. It was Nick. She darted to him.

He grabbed her and held her tight. "What are you

doing out here? You're going to freeze."

She pushed back tears of gratitude welling up inside her. "I heard the scraping then I saw you run into the forest. Obviously, it's the same man who's taunted me since I got here. I worried over what he might do next." She lowered her brows. "Especially to you in the forest."

Nick rubbed Emily's arms. "Yeah. Nothing, but the thing that galls me. He got away. He ran like a deer and then disappeared." He gazed toward the cabin. "He left no clue telling me what he was doing out here."

Nick sounded matter of fact. A façade for her benefit? He must've encountered much worse on his tours overseas. Perhaps chasing after a trespasser *was* all in a night's work for him.

He guided her toward the door. "Hurry inside where you can get warm."

"How about some coffee?"

"Deal." Emily's teeth started to chatter.

Nick whisked her into her country kitchen and started opening the cabinets. "Okay, I found the coffee maker. If you'll put on your yummy brew, I'll build a fire."

"Sounds great." Nick darted to the fireplace.

Out of the wind and icy temperature, she started to warm up. She rubbed her hands together then up and down her arms. Her hands still trembled when put grounds into the coffee maker, causing her to spill some on the counter. Hopefully, she wouldn't get the measurement wrong and ruin their treat. Pfff. She could drink muddy water as long as it was warm.

After fifteen minutes the smell of wood burning wafted in the room.

"Come over by the fire."

Emily did as Nick asked and stood in front of the hot flames. "That was quick. Thank you so much."

"You're welcome."

Emily motioned toward the dining area. "Take a seat and I'll get our drinks."

Still stunned by the events of the evening, by rote she placed cups on two placemats and the glass coffee pot on a hot pad. Then she sat down and directed her attention to Nick. A muscle in his cheek twitched. Was it the mystery surrounding the disappearing trespasser? Or the responsibility of keeping her safe?

As Emily poured Nick's coffee, some dripped down the side of the cup. "Uh, oh." She wiped it. Putting the soiled paper napkin in the wastebasket underneath the sink, she accidentally hit the trashcan. It bumped against something behind it. An object fell with a bang. She recoiled.

Nick shot up and joined Emily. "What was that?"

"I don't know. I think something slipped off of a loose shelf."

They peered inside the cabinet.

A small metal box with numbers on it lay beneath the water pipes. The longer Emily pondered the strange object the weirder it looked. "I have no idea what that is or where it came from."

Nick bent down and studied the item. "If it wasn't so small, I'd say it's a safe. Whoever broke in probably searched for it when he went through the cabinets and your bedroom chest." He pulled a clean dishrag out of a drawer, picked up the mysterious article, and took it to the table.

Emily sat in silence while Nick gave the item the

once over. "Since it was hidden, my guess—the person who put it there probably made sure he didn't leave fingerprints. I'll dust it though. If I find anything to report, I'll contact Sheriff Rivers."

"Shouldn't we at least let him know we found it?"

Nick took a step back. "No, since we have no idea what's inside, who put it under the sink, or why, we have nothing to share."

Emily's mind raced. What did he mean? "Isn't it evidence?"

Nick let out a puff of air. "Possibly."

Emily put her hands on her hips. "Well, if it isn't, I don't know what is."

Nick caressed her shoulder. "One step at a time."

He could afford patience, but could she?

Chapter Eight

Crossing her arms, Emily glanced at the small container on her kitchen table then glared at Nick.

Nick winced. "Come on. I'm going to make sure nothing happens to you."

Finally, a potential clue to solve the mystery of the despicable events ruining her vacation, and Nick wasn't going to tell the authorities. For crying out loud. Emily wanted to scream, but she marched to the counter, reached under the sink, and took hold of the loose shelf hanging by one nail.

"Don't worry. I'll fix that."

It was so much more than a repair job. It was evidence, a lead that could help put an end to her agony. She took a deep sigh. "I'll take you up on the offer."

The two of them moved to the table and sat down in front of the box still lying on the dishcloth. Emily tried to ignore the strange object and focus on her coffee. Still, she couldn't stop gazing at the box. She'd never wanted to see inside a container as much as she did this one, but there was no point in causing an argument.

After all, Nick was trying to help. Considering his background in military intelligence and training for the security guard job, she had to give him the benefit of a doubt. She could take care of herself, but the support meant so much, such a welcome contrast to Donnie. Nagged by questions about the contents of the mysterious find, she refused to let the subject die. "I have an idea. After you dust it, let's find the name of the company that made it, get the model number, and contact a store that sells them. Maybe they can tell us who bought the small safe, or whatever it is."

"That's a great idea. They might hire you to work in the sheriff's office before this is over."

Satisfied Nick was at least open to suggestion, Emily relaxed. "I don't think so. I'll stick to reporting crimes rather than solving them." She cocked an eyebrow. "Uh, well, unless I'm a potential victim."

Nick tilted his head and studied the box from a different angle. "It appears custom made, so it's possible the seller would remember the buyer." Nick winked at Emily. "If he or she used a credit card, we're in business. Neither the manufacturer nor the model number are on the outside. Maybe they're inside."

Emily fanned herself. "I want to open it."

"I understand. I do too, but first things first. If there are fingerprints, it could lead us to the suspect as well as other key players in this clandestine behavior. We can't ignore that." Nick pointed toward the strange focus of their attention. "If it's put together like a safe, it could take forever to crack the combination."

Emily placed her palms on the table. "Please don't tell me we found something to stop the madness, but we can't see it."

"Don't worry. Think positive. I know another way." Nick raised his brows. "We're only getting started."

She liked the conviction in Nick's tone. "Okay, but how? Were you suggesting you can open it without the code?"

"It looks like a digital safe. If that's so, I won't have a problem." He eyed the box from several directions. "I have to check it out to make sure. I'm going right now to dust this thing for prints. I don't expect the trespasser will return tonight. Get some sleep and meet me in the office tomorrow at 9:00 a.m."

"Okay. If only we can find out what's in there."

"Count on it," Nick declared before he left.

~

Nick wanted to take Emily in his arms and tell her not to worry, to let her know he would keep her safe. His desire to protect her and the urgency to find out the contents of the container tied his insides in knots. The first time he saw Emily, something drew him to her. He didn't understand it. No woman had impressed him in any way except as another human being since Caroline died.

Emily fascinated him like the sun dancing on a lake's surface. He wasn't sure if it was her beauty, but he didn't think so. Her strength in spite of her vulnerable situation puzzled him. And her determined spirit. Rather than wait on help from trained professionals, she would go to great lengths to keep a possible murderer from invading her life. He would get to know her better, but he had to solve this mystery first.

He'd kept a finger printing kit ever since an MP gave him his first one when he was in the military. He laid the small object on his kitchen table, retrieved the brush, and dusted the container. There was something important, secret in that miniature safe.

His fingers itched to get this thing open, but his eyelids kept closing as though someone pulled them down like shades. His list of work and school related tasks lay heavy on him. The last thing he wanted to do—make a mistake and ruin a possible clue. Sleep. Precious sleep.

He went to the bedroom, which had knotty pine walls and smelled a little musty despite his best efforts at cleaning. Ah, the light blue and dark green comforter appeared as though it had never been used. Fully clothed, he turned back the coverlet and plopped on the bed, cutting zzz's in no time.

He missed the alarm and woke at eight forty-five. He jumped up, shaved, showered and grabbed the tiny safe. Trying to make it to the office before Emily waited too long, he stepped at a fast pace. This time of year, no one, except an occasional forest ranger, who joined Nick for morning coffee, showed up before eleven o'clock. The mailman didn't come until one or two in the afternoon. He found Emily waiting for him though.

He waved and struck his best smile as he approached the porch. "Good morning, seems I overslept." He chuckled. Maybe that's good though. You're here in time to brew our coffee if you wouldn't mind."

"I'm more than happy to."

Nick opened the door, and they went inside. A gray ambiance hovered over the room until he opened the blinds and sunlight brought the place to life. They hung their coats on a hall tree, and Nick pointed to the refreshment stand. "Yours is much better than mine."

"Okay, you don't need to flatter me. I'm glad to make our morning pick me up." Emily grinned.

Nick placed the safe on his desk and sat down. Emily joined him, slid her chair close, and leaned forward. "So, what about fingerprints?"

"No, I'm sorry to say."

Emily leaned back. "That's too bad, but you are going to open it, right?"

Nick couldn't wait to discover the contents. "Yes, all isn't lost. I believe it's a digital safe, even though it's a little different from most safes I've seen…"

"Why have you seen safes?"

Nick guffawed. "I'm not a robber if that's on your mind. When I was in military intelligence, I dealt with safes from time to time."

"Whew! That's a relief."

"Come on now. You don't really think I could rob someone." He leaned toward her. "Do you?"

Emily fidgeted with her sweater sleeve. "No. I guess after everything that's happened—first at my wedding, and now this…" She was going to say she'd lost faith in humanity in general.

"I get it. You're a bit jittery, and your brain rushes to conclusions."

Emily let go of the sweater and glanced up. "I hadn't thought about it that way, but yes. It's that obvious, huh?"

"Nah, I've been there." Having Caroline die while he was overseas, Nick made so many assumptions. It took a long time, but he finally realized his worst one— it wouldn't have happened if he'd been there—wasn't true. Out of nowhere it seemed, Caroline got cancer. He couldn't have prevented her illness. Nonetheless, guilt still plagued him because he wasn't with her toward the end. He couldn't think about that now. A purpose beyond going through the motions of living needed his attention. He wouldn't fail this challenge. "But, back to work." He studied the item as though getting it open was a matter of life and death.

~

Emily wanted to make sure he understood the small container was critical. "Whatever's in there is probably important, or someone wouldn't have secured it."

"I agree. Since it isn't attached to a wall, I've sized up the design as best I can. I'm going to try the bounce method."

Emily couldn't imagine what he was talking about, but he was the expert. "Hey, whatever works."

"I need to take it into the manager's living area. You're welcome to come or wait here."

"Go ahead. I'm fine here."

"I'll come right back."

Nick left and Emily gazed around the room. Pictures of people having fun kayaking on the river, picnicking at the waterfall, and hiking on a trail with lush trees and green shrubs as well as pink and white flowers showed pleasant times at Sky High—like the ones she remembered.

Nick returned swinging the container in one hand and a small device in the other. "Success. It *is* a tiny safe, and..." he raised the item. "This flash drive was inside. I can't wait to see what's on it." He darted to the computer, sat down, and inserted the memory stick. As he studied the screen, his facial muscles drooped until his jaws looked like a Basset Hound's. "I can't read it." He pushed up his sweater sleeves and scooted closer to the machine. "I *will* figure it out." He stared at the screen with a helpless look. "I think this thing's too old."

"Let's try my laptop. It's at the cabin."

Nick sprang up and yanked out the USB drive. "Okay."

He grabbed his coat and rushed out of the office, Emily on his heels. When they reached the cabin, in a record eight minutes, they went straight to her computer on the kitchen table. Nick sat down and turned it on. Emily held her breath as he inserted the flash drive. A drawing resembling a map filled the screen. Odd. It had no road designations, rivers, towns, nothing except names written on particular spots.

Nick studied it until a distant gaze filled his eyes.

The name at the bottom of the line read *two bears*; a bit farther up, *painted rock*. The path curved and eventually ended back near *two bears*. At the peak of the drawing someone had written *dancing tree*. About a half-inch before reaching two bears again the circle protruded and read *rushing water*. Emily took a step back. "I have no idea how to follow this."

Nick wiggled the mouse. "Even though the titles are direct and straight forward, this type of map, if it is a map, tells us nothing. I'm not even sure if it shows this area. Sheriff Rivers knows a lot about the history of Western North Carolina. I'll call and ask if I can bring over the flash drive."

Concerned, Emily asked, "Do you have gas?"

"Yes, it isn't far. I filled up right before they ran out."

"I'd like to go with you and find out what we're up against."

Chapter Nine

Emily gazed out the window on the way to Broken Arrow. Looking at the mountains in the distance reaching toward Heaven inspired her. She would stay strong like one of these hills no matter what happened.

When they arrived at Sheriff Rivers' office, Nick parked in front of the rustic, wood framed building and led Emily inside. A small, nearly deserted room with straight back chairs lined two walls. In the back, a red-haired receptionist sat behind a wall with a cutout with bars over it. As Emily walked toward the lady, she whispered to Nick, "This reminds me of buying tickets at a movie theatre, except the open area has bars instead of plastic in front of it. A foreboding aura surrounds it."

Nick chuckled. "The precautions are meant to protect the innocent and intimidate the criminals." He walked up to the greeter. "Hi Rachel, how's everything in Broken Arrow?"

"It's quiet here like we like it. How about the campground?"

"Not as peaceful as we want. That's why I called Sheriff Rivers."

"He told me to expect you."

"Good. This is Emily Hanover." He motioned toward Rachel. "Rachel Winters."

Emily and Rachel exchanged greetings.

Then Rachel left her post and joined them. "Follow me."

She escorted them to an entryway on the right side of the lobby and inserted a code. "It's all the way to the end." After they walked past several closed doors, she cracked one and peeked inside. "Sheriff Rivers, they're here."

"Send them in," a gravelly voice replied.

Rachel opened the portal and motioned toward a medium-sized room with cream-colored walls and three rows of filing cabinets.

A distinguished looking man with broad shoulders and high cheekbones rose. A bit of gray dusted his short, dark hair at the temples. He reached across a black, L-shaped computer desk and shook Emily and Nick's hands. "Have a seat."

After they sat down Sheriff Rivers took his seat. "Let's see what you've got."

Nick gave the sheriff the flash drive.

Sheriff Rivers inserted it and brought up the information on his screen. Staring with intensity, he said, "Hmm." Within five minutes, he wrote on a pad, pulled out the memory stick and handed it to Nick. "So, what's happening over there?"

"Suspicious activity, sir." Nick glanced at Emily. "The first night she arrived she heard strange noises as though someone hit or scraped rock. When she looked outside, she believed she saw a man carrying a dead body. Also, we found a hole about three feet deep beside a large boulder."

Sheriff Rivers shot straight up. "A dead body? I can't remember the last time we had a corpse that didn't die of natural causes around here."

"Well, I know. That's what I told her. I inspected the yard and concluded an animal turned over the trashcans. I figured one of the forest people, possibly a veteran with a brain injury got confused and thought he dug a grave, or maybe a hunter who killed a deer carried it across her yard."

Sheriff Rivers nodded. "Uh, huh. Sounds reasonable."

"But there's more. Someone broke into her cabin and took nothing. I decided to move into the unit next door. The very next night I chased off a man who trespassed on her front yard." The muscle in Nick's jaw bunched. "I intended to catch him, but he gave me the slip in the forest…" Nick slapped his palm on Sheriff Rivers' desk. "…where I found, not one, but two holes."

Sheriff Rivers knitted his brows. "I see. Now, you don't think the person in her yard was one of our forest people. You believe the flash drive and the man you ran after are connected."

Nick sat back. "Correct."

Sheriff Rivers steepled his fingers. "All right, so tell me about the flash drive."

Nick explained about the shelf nearly falling out from under the sink when Emily hit it with the trashcan.

"That was a stroke of luck. I don't think you'd ever have looked under there." Sheriff Rivers scooted to the edge of his seat. "Apparently, neither did the suspect." He folded his arms over his chest. "Unfortunately, I have no clue about two bears or the dancing tree mentioned, but there's a huge boulder with a picture on it in the woods. It's faded now, but romanticists say it was a yesteryear spot for picnics. Others claim it was a marker for hunters."

A clue. Finally. Emily nearly sprang out of her seat for wanting to locate the rock right now. "What does the image look like?"

"Not much today. Some of the colors remain from the early painting of a branch with green leaves and a purple mountain laurel blossom."

Nick leaned forward. "We'll examine that for sure."

Sheriff Rivers tapped his fingers on his desk. "That is definitely not a map drawn by a cartographer. I'd say whoever put it together intended to point out one of our waterfalls."

Nick hopped up. "Thank you."

Sheriff Rivers stood. "You're welcome. Let me know if you need anything else."

"I will."

When they left the sheriff, Nick headed to the manager's office at the campground. Going forty miles an hour, he said, "I'm driving at a slow, steady pace to preserve as much fuel as possible."

"Great idea." Emily sat back in the passenger's seat and peered out the window. "I'm enjoying the scenery. I can't wait to find the painted rock though."

"That makes two of us. We'll start looking as soon as possible."

Nick pulled into the gravel parking lot at the office and cut the engine. "We only used one-quarter of a tank of gas."

"Thank goodness," Emily said.

After they went inside, Emily pulled a chair up to

Nick's desk and sat down. "I think Sheriff Rivers believes there's more to this situation than a forest person wandering around."

"I agree. That's why he said he would help."

Nick straightened papers on his desk. During his military days, he kept his documents in meticulous order. The habit had stayed with him. Seeing a note from Larry stuck in with printed information obtained from the flash drive, he bristled. He picked it up. Umm. About the light bill. He'd already taken care of it. He checked his inbox, which held only a few papers and envelopes. "There's almost nothing happening here this time of year. I'm anxious to find the boulder and rushing water. If no one needs anything by the time the mail comes, I'll open it to see if there's anything important I should mention to Larry. If not, I'll leave." He sat down. "You're welcome to stay as long as you like, but if you have something else to do, I'll come get you if you like."

"Sounds good. I'll look for you this afternoon. I can't wait to follow our first lead."

"I wouldn't put you in danger, but I know you are as anxious as I am to find a clue to start nailing this guy. After all, we're only looking for a rock with a picture. If our ventures grow more dangerous, I may take Sheriff Rivers up on his offer."

Emily intended to stay after the man she believed murdered someone and tried to bury him in her yard, probably the same one who broke into her cabin. To say she was relieved Nick and Sheriff Rivers finally believed her was an understatement. Yet, she still had more at stake than either of them. She was the target. "As you know, I'm already at risk. I appreciate the sentiment though." Emily left Nick studying the map.

She enjoyed a cool, brisk walk to the cabin, where she ate a grilled cheese sandwich and sipped a glass of sweet tea, one of her cooking specialties. She held up the glass and a fond memory flashed in her mind.

When her mother taught her to make Southern sweet tea, she told her after she boiled and steeped the tea bags, she would need sugar and lemon juice. Emily asked, "How much sugar?" Her mother promptly walked over and turned up a bag of sweetener. As far as Emily could tell, she poured one and one-half cups into the pitcher. "Put it in there until it looks right, like this."

Emily couldn't help but laugh out loud. Everyone enjoyed her tea. When Nick came later, she would offer him some. With the image of her and Mom making tea and one of Nick flashing in her brain right behind it, she realized she had made it all morning without thinking about Donnie leaving her at the altar. Not only that, his name just popped in her mind and she didn't grow nauseated or weak. Maybe this vacation was serving its purpose in spite of the unexpected stress.

She finished the tea and picked up her eReader, but all she could think about was the painted rock, rushing water, and what they would tell her and Nick.

Chapter Ten

Emily let Nick inside the cabin at six o'clock as the sun gave way to twilight.

He stood at the doorway and spread his arms wide. "The mail was late today. Then, Larry called. I had to stay and talk with him about plans for my Spring Break and this summer."

Emily peeped outside. "It's perfect timing. We'll have enough light to see with a bit of cover as long as the sky stays gray." She grabbed a flashlight and her door key, and they left.

When they reached the edge of the forest, the vast landscape looked like a giant maze with the hills dotted with barren trees, which seemed to go as far as she could see. "Which way should we go?"

Nick stopped. "I have no idea." He scanned the vast area. "We have to start somewhere. Let's walk to the two holes and go from there."

Nick strode at a quick pace, Emily staying with him step for step. She couldn't wait to turn proof over to the sheriff, sit back, and enjoy the mountain views. "Good idea. He must've had a reason to dig in that particular spot. Maybe it represents two bears."

"I don't know. I suppose it's possible." He looped

his arm around Emily's elbow as if to guide her along, which he did until they needed to switch to single file.

When he let go and slipped behind her, she missed his grasp and it dawned on her. His touch gave her a sense of security she'd never known with Donnie even in the best of times, and these were scary times. She looked to her left then her right without seeing much except green underbrush, bare tree trunks and withered, brown grass waiting for spring to clothe it in color until…until…she halted and pointed. "Hey, I think they're over there."

Nick squinted as he looked that way. "You're right. Good job."

"These holes don't look like bears to me, but maybe they are a signal to someone." Emily rubbed the toe of her shoe around the ground. "Where do we go from here?"

Nick peered into the distance. "Let's stay on a straight path. It's as good of a guess as any for now."

They started their trek again. When evening turned to night, they switched on their flashlights. Geez. They'd be lucky to see something as big as the Brooklyn Bridge. With few stars out and little light from the moon tonight only two flashlights lit their trail. Yet, they hadn't gone more than twenty feet when Emily spotted it. She ran to the rock. "Here. Here. It's right here."

In moments Nick stood beside her, both of them staring at splotches and specks of purple, green, and brown paint.

Nick rubbed the granite. "I wonder what this means to the man who's been digging holes." He stepped closer and inspected the specks of paint. Then he focused his flashlight from the top to the bottom. Repeating the process, he walked all the way around the boulder. "I don't see anything unusual here."

He groaned. "We've assumed this stone and the other landmarks are places to conceal an object, or they form a path leading to a hidden location. What if two bears, painted rock, dancing tree, and rushing water are starting points? Say the trespasser wants to find something, he could end up at any of the four locations, but he has information that tells him where to go from each spot." Nick clasped his hands behind his back. "What if he needs the flash drive to find the markers?"

Emily mentally pieced together the information. "You're saying someone's roaming these hills to seize an item. He knows what it is but not where it is." The answer to why the man dug in her yard seemed so obvious. "The man came in my cabin looking for the flash drive, but who did he murder, and why did he need to off them?"

"There's a good chance whatever's out there is stolen, illegal, or payment for illegal services. There's no other reason the trespasser would take such drastic measures. At least not one I can think of. We have to find whatever he's after before he does. And we will." The strength of steel resounded in his voice.

"Okay, what next? Wait. I hear something."

"Quick, get behind the rock." Nick pulled Emily into place, and they switched off their flashlights.

Someone whistled. The melody grew louder. Emily's brain raced with questions she couldn't answer. Did forest people use whistling for a code among them? If not, who was whistling? Why was he out here? To bury a body?

"Stay very quiet, and whatever you do, don't move," Nick whispered.

"I'm not even breathing."

The shrill notes drifted over the top of them. Emily pushed her fingernails into her palms.

Silence fell.

"All right, I believe I'm at the painted rock," the whistler said.

Emily's pulse throbbed in her temples.

Beams from a flashlight crept toward her, and Nick moved right then left. Emily sank back against him. He pulled her forward to get her out of the light. She clutched her fists tighter with each tug. Could he take her to safety?

He dragged her to a large oak tree and lined her up against it. Nick stood against the tree next to her and shot her reassuring glances. A stick broke. Nick gave her an intense stare. She inhaled and exhaled slowly.

The whistler swung the light toward their new hideaway, moving it in sweeping lines while he held the phone to his ear.

Emily stiffened. *Please Lord, protect us.*

"I thought I heard something over near some trees. I'm going to take a look see."

Emily pushed against the tree she leaned on with all her might, both to hide and to keep upright.

Silence.

"I will. I want to see who's out here."

Emily swallowed to keep from vomiting.

"All right. No," the voice hollered. "I'm not the problem. I can stay on task. The problem is you keep sending me where there ain't nothin.' You said the flash drive was in that cabin."

Emily's heart beat so hard she feared the man talking on the cell phone heard it.

"Well, let me tell you, I went over that place like a vacuum cleaner. There ain't no flash drive in there. I know I'm wandering around in the dark without it. I'm out here every night looking for the stuff with no direction. I'm getting tired of it. I want my money."

Silence.

"Yeah, you're right. It might make the job go quicker if I left here to examine the rest of the rock, but I'm telling you there's someone out here. What? An elk? Yeah, I *seen* one of 'em in these woods a few days ago, but I ain't lookin' at one right now."

Emily's hands grew clammy.

"What? A squirrel? Naw, it ain't no squirrel. I know what they sound like runnin' around. Hold on. I think I see a raccoon coming out of a hollowed-out tree trunk. I thought they hibernated."

Silence.

"Torpor? Naw, I never heard of no inactive torpor state below fifteen, but it's not *that* cold out here."

Emily could hardly breathe. Why couldn't he just shut up and leave?

"All right. I'm going to finish looking around the rock. The noise must've been one of *them* raccoons that ain't gone into torpor because it's not cold enough."

He walked away.

Emily sat down, waiting in the dark, cold night for thirty minutes for the forest to grow quiet.

When it finally did, Nick joined her. "You're shivering." He pulled her to him, and she fell into his arms.

He held her tight. "It's okay. He's gone. I need to

think through all of this, but first, let's go to the cabin where it's warm. Are you alright to walk?"

"Of course." Emily's legs were as weak as half-steeped tea, but she would never say that. She couldn't leave fast enough. She dug deep inside seeking God's help and found the strength to walk, even picking up her pace when she saw the porch light.

After they got in the cabin, they took off their coats and went to the kitchen. Nick brushed together his hands then blew on them while Emily rubbed her arms, quivering from the cold, and partly from fear, she had to admit. "Brrr," she said.

"Right, do you still have some of that good herbal blend coffee?"

"Yes, I'll get it." Emily reached in the cabinet with a shaky hand while Nick sat down at the table.

"Do you have a pen and paper?"

"Yep. Right here." She pulled them from a drawer and gave them to him then finished preparing the brew.

The heat started to penetrate Emily's pores as the aroma of hazelnut filled the room. She glanced at Nick, and a cozy aura formed around her. Finally, she started to unwind. After she poured their drinks and set them down, she joined him. "I'm getting warm at last."

"Me too." He sipped his coffee. "Heavenly."

"I'm glad you like it." Emily ran her finger up and down the handle of the cup. "Uh, with the military training you have, I thought you might tackle the guy and ask questions later."

Nick cracked his knuckles. "I wanted to. It took all of the restraint I had to keep from hitting him. I realize it's more important to find out what he's up to and who's behind it. If he thinks someone is on to him, we probably won't see any more of him. Right now, he's our only link to the people behind what's really going on. We have to remain patient."

Emily patted his shoulder. "You're good at investigation."

He tapped his spoon on the table. "We'll see about that, but I appreciate the vote of confidence. I promise you I'll do the best I can to get all we need to nail this guy. I can't wait to find out whose body he's been carrying around and why."

"One thing we know for sure—he doesn't have the flash drive." Emily tilted her head. "Beyond that, I can't put the pieces together. I know I saw him with a dead body."

"I don't have a clue who it might have been, or how that person ended up a corpse, but I know you're telling the truth. I'll share our information with Sheriff Rivers. Unfortunately, so far, we can't tell him who this man is, what he's doing, or why he's doing it. What's worse, we don't even have the body."

Emily hit the table with her fist. "I know what I saw."

Nick leaned closer to Emily. "Hey, I know you did. I just agreed with you." He ran his hand through his hair. "Let me rephrase that. We don't have the location of the body."

Emily breathed in and exhaled. *Better.*

"If there's a body out here..." Nick held up his hand. "Don't say it. I said that wrong too. I believe there is a body out here, and *I will find it.* But we can't do anymore tonight. Let's talk again tomorrow."

"Okay."

After Emily gave Nick his coat, he lingered gazing

at her with a longing look.

Emily put her hands over her cheeks to camouflage her attraction for him, but her fascination with him crept from her heart. Trying to discern whether or not she'd hidden it successfully, she glanced at him.

He had a closed-mouth grin.

If they were outside, she'd crawl into the hole in her yard. She took a step back.

Finally, Nick looked away. "Well, goodnight. Get some rest."

He shut the door and left. Emily locked it and pondered what just happened between them as she walked to the bedroom.

She pulled her nightgown over her head, slipped underneath the covers, and turned out the lamp on the nightstand. The blackness sent a wave of shivers over her. She got up and switched on a nightlight, but once she got back under the covers, she thought about Nick staying next door and comfort settled her. Whatever happened, he'd take care of it. She sat straight up. Wouldn't he?

Chapter Eleven

Nick took lighter steps to the manager's office. He believed the sun shined brighter today, but admitted he probably thought that because he had gotten a good night's sleep. It would serve him well as he attempted to unravel the mystery plaguing Sky High Campground. Emily had been right all along. There was more to the holes in her yard and the woods than strange noises and digging. That set his nerves on edge for her.

He kicked a rock. He didn't believe for one instant the culprit wanted to hurt Emily, unless she got in his way, or she was in the wrong place at the wrong time. Why not move her?

Nick took quick steps. He'd look for a different cabin as soon as he got to the office. No. Wait. That wouldn't help. Who knew where this guy would search for the flash drive next?

It was his responsibility to make sure the tourists at the campground stayed safe, but with Emily it ran deeper. It had taken him by surprise. After Caroline he never intended to get involved with anyone else. She had been the only one for him, and…He squished his eyebrows together and focused off in the distance. And all of a sudden out of nowhere Emily appeared. Before he had time to think about it, he cared for her.

His friend, Sam, who had known Caroline, believed in love at first sight and in second chances. Nick always had thought Sam didn't know what he was talking about because he hadn't experienced the depth of loss and pain Nick had, but maybe Sam was right. He had said, "You're young and have lots to offer. Remember, you're here. You need to keep going, not grieve your life away. One of these days, you'll see a woman who pulls on your heart like a magnet." Sam flattered him saying he had a lot to offer, but he was on target saying a woman would get to him. He would give his best to Emily. Affection for her fell over him like stars. Before he could do anything about it, he had to rid their lives of the man harassing her.

He answered emails about spring events at Sky High, tidied up his desk, set the phone to voicemail, and left the office, locking the door behind him. Clues left by the elusive hole digger and home invader would show up better in broad daylight.

He hadn't walked ten feet until he ran into Emily. Seeing her, his insides knotted for fear she'd had another incident in the cabin after he left. As she grew closer, he could see her smile.

"Hi, can I help you with something?" he called out.

She picked up her pace until she stood in front of him. "No, no. Everything's fine. I just, you know, I wondered if you'd heard anything, or if Sheriff Rivers could shed any light on the situation."

"All's quiet in the office. I haven't called Sheriff Rivers yet. I'm on my way to look around that painted rock and the area where the holes are."

Emily took a step back. "Hmm. Would you like

company?"

He didn't want to take her into dangerous territory. She probably was better off with him than she was alone though.

"Please, I'll make sandwiches. We'll have a picnic."

Picnic? He was trying to catch a potential killer. As he started to object and explain, his throat tightened. He wanted her with him.

"I can help. You know, crime reporters observe people, surroundings, and objects closely, or at least I do. Obviously, I'm not a surveillance security guard or military intelligence officer, but I might surprise you and find something."

Obviously, she wanted to prove she could contribute to the investigation. Today's task was no more than a hike with them looking for a painted rock. He'd watch out for her. He put his hand on his stomach. He hadn't eaten today.

"It's a bright, sunshiny day. This guy usually comes to my cabin in the middle of the night or the wee hours of the morning."

He leaned back and looked up. She even knew the guy's MO. "Okay, but you have to do everything I say."

She jerked to attention and saluted.

He couldn't help but laugh and she giggled.

He walked her to her cabin where she hurriedly put together sandwiches, grabbed paper plates and plastic utensils and poured tea into a large thermos.

She snatched up the picnic basket and the drink. "We're ready."

Nick guided her out the cabin door. He had to admit, his day grew brighter. The dazzling picnic partner swung her basket as rays of sunshine glistened on the forest and opened his senses to the beauty around him. No matter where they walked, they found leafless trees, pines with green needles, and underbrush dotted with an occasional winter blossom as though someone ran the foliage through a copy machine. A person could get lost out here. He could not let Emily out of his sight.

They arrived at the painted rock and circled it several times.

Emily studied it. "There's something important about this stone." She stamped her feet. "I can't spot it."

He understood her frustration. "Me either. I pronounce this a marker."

"Agreed."

Nick gazed at the granite. "We have the entire afternoon to scour the woods. Let's eat while we decide what to do next."

"Okay, you know best. Where would you like to sit? I suppose if we're talking fine dining, we could include a nice view."

I know best? Nick's pulse quickened. She finally trusted him, at least for now. "I consider eating anywhere with you fine dining."

Emily's eyes sparkled. "Ah, that's nice. Thank you."

Nick tilted his chin up. Emily's acceptance of him meant more than he'd realized. "You're welcome. There are picnic tables beside the creek." He bit his bottom lip. "Since we want to start searching here as soon as possible, let's sit on that log." He pointed to their right then Emily walked to the large fallen tree trunk with him.

In minutes she pulled out the sandwiches and poured the tea. When Nick took a sip of his drink, he couldn't believe how good it tasted. "Wow! This is the best tea I've ever had."

"My mom taught me how to make it."

Her mom must've shared a secret that made her tea better than most.

"I'm glad you're enjoying it."

Nick held out his paper cup. "Here's to Mom."

Emily followed Nick's gesture. "I'll tell her you like it."

He glanced at Emily and fondness for her filled him. He forgot the vandalism, the holes, and the possible corpse. "Please do. I'd like to meet her someday."

Emily smoothed the front of her coat. "That would be nice."

Content with himself and Emily's reply, Nick finished his sandwich and held out his hand to her. "If you're through eating, I'll put the trash in the picnic basket, but I'll keep my cup." He flashed her a big smile. "I may want more tea, so hang onto it."

"You got it."

They cleaned up and Nick stood. Seeing the forest, recalling the human threat living somewhere in it, brought him back to the reason they came here. "Back to work."

~

Emily walked around the painted boulder searching for a message she couldn't find.

Nick peered down at her. "We've covered this rock and the area around it like a couple of hawks looking for lunch. If anyone left anything here, it's gone. He patted the stone. I don't see anything resembling a code or directions. I might re-visit this place later, but for now let's locate the rushing water." Nick glanced at his watch. "We have a couple of hours of daylight left." He motioned to the right toward a steep hill. "There's a waterfall. According to Sheriff Rivers, there are quite a few, but since this one's right in front of us, let's take a look."

Emily glanced at the cascade. This was a big forest to say the least. The names on the drawing were their only directions for finding whatever the man shoveling holes searched for. Yet, discovering the hiding place was a challenge they needed to win. "Okay."

"We'll scan the pathway as we go."

Emily nodded, slowed her pace, and studied their trail while they pressed on in silence. When they started over a brook, Nick took her hand. Even though she was perfectly capable of navigating the slick rocks, when he wrapped his fingers around her hand, reassurance swept over her like heat from a warm fire.

The sun shining on water spilling over large boulders made the droplets sparkle like liquid diamonds. Emily couldn't imagine anything wicked touching it, but evil could seep into any corner. She directed her gaze to the brook and picked up a piece of paper floating downstream. As they stepped on the ground on the other side, she held it up.

"What have you got there?"

A clue? Emily experienced a moment of excitement shooting through her like electricity. When she got a good look at her find, disappointment crushed her spirits. "It's a bubble gum wrapper."

"That's all right." A reassuring tone lined Nick's

words. He took a paper bag out of his coat pocket and opened it. "Put it in here."

Emily blinked. "You want it?"

"You never know the significance of something. I'll dust it for fingerprints, even though they probably washed away. I leave no bubble gum wrapper uninspected."

Emily chuckled. "That kit you have comes in handy."

"Yep. That's why I kept it."

As they grew closer to the waterfall, the spray splashed on the rocky hill. Emily stepped back to avoid getting wet and stood in awe of the view. "These mountains are breathtaking."

Nick rolled his thick shoulders backward. "Yes, but for now we need to go over this place like two bloodhounds."

"Woof?"

Nick laughed and flicked Emily's nose with his finger. "You'd make an out-of-this-world cute bloodhound."

"I'll take that as a compliment, even though I've never thought I have any canine in my DNA."

Horror flashed over Nick's countenance. "Sorry. My bad. I meant…never mind. You're a gorgeous woman." He gave her that longing look, took a step toward her, and wrapped his arms around her, kissing her like Donnie never had as the roar of the waterfall drowned out the rest of the world.

When he let go, it took several minutes for her to remember anything but the warmth of Nick's embrace.

He hugged her. "We should get to work."

His voice brought her back to reality. She continued

to peruse the land alongside the brook. Another piece of paper. Was there any point in picking it up? Sure, why not? These woods had to hold clues. Maybe this time she'd found one. She stared at it. "Look." She pulled on Nick's jacket sleeve and pointed to her prize. "There's a curvy line with an arrow on it, probably nothing. Maybe a kid dropped it." She started to pick it up.

"No. Kids aren't up here this time of year. Let me get it though." He pulled a handkerchief out of his pants pocket. After he grasped the paper with the cloth, he stared at it with interest. "You know, this looks like the map on the flash drive without the designated points, but what if…"

"Yes, what if?"

"The arrow points to the place where the body's buried, or something connected to it?"

"I hope and pray it does."

"Me too. Let's call off the search and compare this to the map." Enthusiasm rang in his words. "If they match and I can lift fingerprints off of this…" He looked down at the handkerchief and paper, which he clutched in his hand. "We have a place to start."

Emily tilted her chin upward. She had given them a spark of hope. If only Nick could lift the prints.

Chapter Twelve

Standing at the rustic desk in the manager's office Emily leaned over Nick's shoulder, peered at the computer screen, and tried to make sense of the map. "Can you enlarge the copy and lay the piece of paper over it?"

"Yeah."

Emily straightened up. "Wait. What about fingerprints?"

Nick shook his head. "I couldn't get any. I think too many squirrels and raccoons walked across it before we got to it."

Emily placed her hand on her cheek. "If the intruder already had the map, why did he break into the cabin?"

"My guess, since the diagram's so cryptic, he questions it's accuracy." Nick shrugged. "He probably thinks whoever gave the paper version to him, either inadvertently or on purpose, fed him the wrong information."

"Hmm. I hadn't thought of that, but I bet you're right."

In moments Nick made the adjustment and sure enough, the marks on the paper fit right over the ones on the map. "An arrow lines up with the words two bears." He tapped the computer screen. "Tomorrow I'm going to take all of this to Sheriff Rivers and see what he thinks. In the meantime…" He flashed Emily a flirty grin. "Why don't we go out to dinner?"

Emily wasn't sure if he invited her to accommodate their investigation, if he wanted to establish a friendship, or more, but she was all for it. "Sounds good to me."

Nick and Emily walked to Sky High Pizza, a popular tourist spot that stayed open year around.

Emily savored the cozy atmosphere with cheery, red and white checked tablecloths and a fire in a rock fireplace, which replaced the day's anxiety with cozy warmth. Sitting across from Nick in the glow of candlelight listening to Italian music sent a romantic aura over her. How unlikely she would find the peace she had yearned for when she came here amid the aroma of tomato sauce and oregano, but she had, and more.

The waitress brought a large pizza oozing with cheese and pepperoni to share and Emily bit into a piece.

Nick leaned forward. "How is it?"

Emily wiped her mouth with the red, linen napkin. "Yum. Best I've ever had." That was because she was with Nick, but she didn't say that.

He chuckled, took a slice then sipped his soda. After a couple more servings, he sat back in his seat. "We needed this. No one can work twenty-four hours a day…" He scooted to the edge of his chair. "That might be an exaggeration. Not by much though."

They laughed.

All too soon, as far as Emily was concerned, they

finished, and Nick paid. They left, and drove through the sleepy, little town with its two-lane road lit by lampposts. The craft shop, the drugstore, and a grocery lined the tranquil street in a valley. Lights flickered in the homes nestled into the hillside above them, making the place look like a twinkling paradise set apart from the evils of the world. Emily sighed. It wasn't though.

Gravel crunching underneath Nick's tires broke the silence of the still night as he pulled up in front of Emily's cabin. After they entered, he put his arm around her waist. "Wait until I make sure the place is secure before you go any farther."

A protective military guy. Yeah, that was nice.

He ambled out of sight down the hall and returned smiling. "There's no one here but us." With regret washing over his countenance he said, "I have to get to the office early tomorrow, so I need to go next door and turn in. I don't think anyone will come around here again. The trespasser has already inspected the place and didn't find anything. It only makes sense for him to look somewhere else." He gave Emily a sweet kiss and left.

Emily wasn't sure Nick was right about the threat, but one thing was gone for sure—the shame and grief of Donnie's rejection. Now it seemed it had occurred in another lifetime. It had only been a couple of months since Donnie left her at the altar, but coming to the campground and meeting Nick put her relationship with Donnie in perspective. Even if nothing ever came of knowing Nick after spending time with him, she saw Donnie in a different light.

She wanted to give Donnie the benefit of a doubt, say they simply weren't meant for each other. He would find someone and treat her well, but deep down she didn't believe that. The way she saw it, the Lord kept her from making a big mistake. Nick unintentionally taught her a lot more than how to test for fingerprints.

She would see Nick tomorrow. She needed to wash her favorite blouse, the white one with tiny green leaves on it. She grabbed the laundry and threw it in the washing machine then plopped down at the kitchen table, spread her fingers apart, painted her nails, and blew on them. "There."

She stood in front of the mirror trying to decide what to do with her hair tomorrow. After pulling it back then flipping it over her shoulders, she settled on putting it up with ringlets hanging by her cheeks. Nick had only seen her with her hair hanging down without any style to it, or pulled back in a ponytail, but tomorrow he'd see a different her. She put on pajamas and curled up in the bed.

In the wee hours of the morning banging woke her. She sprang up. Quivering inside she listened for the next slam. It came from the front porch. She stiffened, but she had to do something—the weirdo was at her cabin again. *Do something. Do something.* Call Nick.

The front door rattled. Emily pressed her fists to the sides of her head. She scanned the bedroom. Where was her phone? She threw her housecoat off of the bed. Pulled back the comforter and yanked off the top sheet. No phone.

Loud scratching.

She switched off the lamp and pulled the flashlight out of the nightstand. On weak legs she wobbled into the bathroom. Screams built inside her and she nearly choked. No phone.

Scratching from the front of the house echoed in her brain like a thousand cats clawing. Shaking, she turned on the flashlight, cupped her hand around it, and tiptoed toward the kitchen. There lay her phone beside her fingernail polish on the table. Anger built inside her. Why did she leave her phone in here? What an idiot. Fear overwhelmed her. She thought she might explode.

A grating noise drifted indoors. She got on her hands and knees and crawled toward the table. Whacks and clanks coming from the door rang in her ears. The flashlight sent erratic splashes of light across the floor. She shined it on the door. The wiggling hinges barely hung on. The knob turned. *Help. Help. Help.* She hollered in her mind as she crept closer to the phone. Finally, she made it to the table. She tried to pull up on a chair. It turned over with a loud thud.

Everything grew quiet. The doorknob stopped moving. Pounding hit the door. Emily flinched with each strike. A hinge broke. On her knees, Emily propped her elbows on the table. Wiggled her fingers toward the phone. They didn't reach. She leaned forward. Got it. But tremors ran through her fingers. She took deep breaths. Finally, she punched speed dial.

Morc pummeling resounded. The other hinge wiggled.

Nick's phone rang, and rang, and rang.

Please pick up.

Finally, Nick's sleepy voice said, "Hello."

"It's me. Someone's breaking in the cabin." The phone fell from Emily's hand as she sank to the floor.

~

Breaking in. Nick bounded out of the bed and hurried so fast to dress his foot stuck at the knee of his pants. He yanked them off and started over, nearly tripping over the bottoms as he stumbled over his shower flip-flops. He regained his balance and wiggled as fast as he could to get the pants on. Grabbing a sweatshirt, he pulled it over his head and ran to the living area. Switched on the porch light and spotlights. Grabbed his Glock 22. Snatched a flashlight. If the perpetrator saw the lights coming on next door, unless he was nuts, he'd flee.

That's exactly what happened. Nick chased a figure into the forest, when all of a sudden, just like last time, the guy disappeared leaving Nick standing in the dark, cold night with question marks floating in his mind. It was as if the man fell into a trapdoor in the earth. Nick canvassed the area searching for an escape route, but he couldn't find one.

He didn't want to frighten Emily any more than this disaster already had, but this was neither a harmless forest person or an ordinary low-life trying to steal a little living money. This was a hardened, slick criminal. Nick would bet his last dollar, the trespasser had high-up connections. When he put all of it together, as he told Emily, the best thing to do was let this creep lead him to the kingpins of the organization. But the thing that mattered most to him was keeping Emily safe.

He'd had little to no sleep since he arrived at Sky High Campground. He was too exhausted to keep running in a haphazard pursuit tonight. He needed to leave and see about Emily. Yet, he was just getting started. He would catch this guy.

He trudged to Emily's cabin, took hold of the door nearly falling off of its hinges, and opened it. The squeaking sent an eerie sound that rattled his bones. As he walked through the ramshackled entryway, he bit his bottom lip until he drew a drop of blood. Emily sat with her hands over her knees and rocked back and forth. He rushed to her, his pulse beating in his temples as he sat down beside her and wrapped his arms around her. "Are you alright?"

She buried her face in his shoulder. "I'm glad to see you."

He pulled her close and held her tight. "Not nearly as glad as I am to see you. I will not let this happen again. I can't believe this man returned after I chased him into the forest the first time."

"Did you get him?" Emily sounded as though she thought her life depended on Nick capturing the man with the shovel.

Nick gritted his teeth. "No, but I will."

She looked up. "Did he run too fast, or shoot at you? I didn't hear any shots."

"No, he just disappears all of a sudden. I never realized the earth had a trapdoor." Sarcasm lined his tone.

Emily gave him a weak snicker. "I don't think it does. Are there any caves he could run into?"

"Possibly. I walked around looking for one, but I will return during daylight and find the black hole he falls into." He hugged Emily again.

"You're shivering. I'll get you a blanket." She got up and walked unsteadily across the floor to a hall closet and returned with a coverlet."

Nick pulled it around his shoulders. "I won't turn it down. Let's sit on the sofa."

Emily leaned on Nick's shoulder and fell asleep. Within minutes, he did too.

When he awoke at six o'clock and headed out the door, Emily was in the kitchen.

"Hold up a second, and I'll get us coffee."

Nick's insides revved like an engine racing. "Uh…"

"I know you have lots to do, but it will only take a minute. It will get you moving."

Nick pulled a chair up to the table. "I can't turn down the morning coffee smell, but I need to sip and leave."

"Right, I'm coming to the office as soon as I can to see if Sheriff Rivers has any news." Emily set the cups on the table and Nick gulped his drink.

"Thanks." He glanced at the flip-flops on his feet. "I'll stop by my cabin, but only long enough to get better shoes."

Emily blinked several times. "You went out in flip-flops? Really? I was so scared I didn't notice."

"I was focused on other stuff too, but it's fine. I'll see you later. I'll send someone to fix the door before the day's end."

Emily let out a soft sigh. "I appreciate it."

"You bet. Come on down when you're ready." The door squeaked again as Nick opened it and left.

Leaving Emily alone with her door half hanging weighed on his conscience. Disapproving of his negligence, he let out a soft growl of disgust at himself. He was ninety-nine percent sure Emily was safe for now. No incidents had occurred during daylight. He would contact the maintenance man as soon as he got to the office then he'd call Sheriff Rivers. Everything would turn out fine. Maybe by the time Emily stopped by, he'd have answers for her.

Even though he hadn't known Emily that long, he

didn't doubt for one minute she would hurry to dress and try to help him solve this mystery because that was who she was, afraid, of course, but driven. Not one to wait and let someone else do it for her. He opened the door to the office as he pondered how he could be so certain what Emily might and might not do.

Odd, maybe some people were more open than others, or maybe he paid more attention to Emily because he wanted to find out all he could about her. He had to admit, she drew him in with a force as strong as a tornado, something he never would have believed could happen.

Knowing Emily was in danger made him want to charge into the woods, kick over every rock and log and knock down trees until he found this guy and ripped him to pieces. Obviously, he couldn't do that. Once he did locate this ne'er-do-well, he better be glad he was a Christian, or he might give in to the anger that boiled in his veins.

Chapter Thirteen

When Emily entered the manager's office, Nick sat staring at his computer screen, wrinkles creasing his brow like rivers on a map.

"Hi." She hoped her cheerful tone would lighten his spirits.

He looked up. "Hey, maintenance is on the way to repair the door. I'm going to report the vandalism to Sheriff Rivers and ask for his support."

Even though Emily wasn't sure if he wanted to let her know he was doing all he could to resolve her trespasser problem or comfort her. She'd take either or both options. "His help would be a blessing. Maybe we could get a good night's sleep."

"I'll second that. If Sheriff Rivers can't make it here this afternoon, I'm going over there. If you want, wait for the carpenter to fix the door, sign his sheet, and come back. I'll take you with me to Broken Arrow, or you're welcome at our meeting in the office."

"Sounds good. See you later." Emily left.

By one o'clock the repairman had come and gone. The door looked as good as new. Emily rushed back to the manager's office and charged through the doorway. "What's the word from Sheriff Rivers?" She asked in ragged breaths.

Nick gave a victory sign. "I think we have his attention. He has more gas than I do, so he's coming here. Do you want to make coffee?"

"Sure." Emily shot to the coffee station. She couldn't wait to do her part to get this meeting underway.

By the time the libation brewed, Sheriff Rivers entered and took a seat at Nick's desk. After Emily served the drinks, she pulled up a chair beside him and sat across from Nick.

Sheriff Rivers took a sip from his cup then placed his palms on the desk. "I realize you have more information to give me now, but let's start from the beginning." He turned toward Emily. "We have enough reserve fuel at the Sheriff's Office to send the Deputy to patrol your cabin at night. Leave spotlights on outside and one or two lights inside."

"Okay, thank you."

"You're welcome. Tell me again what happened your first night here." Sheriff Rivers' cast an interested, intense gaze toward Emily.

For the first time, she sensed he wanted to hear something she had to say. "I heard noises like metal scraping rock. Later Nick and I found the hole in the yard."

Sheriff Rivers nodded. "Yes, we have lots of granite in these hills."

"The mystery man also dug two holes in the woods, but there's not a body in any of them." Emily sweated just saying those words. Would the sheriff understand some cruel man's carrying a dead body around these hills?

"Yeah. Apparently, he had the same problem there. He couldn't dig too far before hitting stone, but go on. What's this about the flash drive and two bears?"

Nick answered Sheriff Rivers' question. "Obviously, the suspect needs the flash drive to locate something. I'm guessing, just guessing mind you, he tried to duplicate the map, maybe from directions he was given verbally, or overheard. I think he grew frustrated when he couldn't find any of the four markers and threw down the map."

Sheriff Rivers' eyes widened. "I'll go along with that." He pushed back his chair and got up, so Nick and Emily did too. He turned toward Nick. "Let's locate two bears and go from there."

Oh no, they don't. They are not leaving me out of this. Emily put her hands on her hips. "What about me?"

"We can't allow you to get involved."

Emily shook her head. "You can't be serious. I'm already involved. I don't want to stay on the entire campground by myself with a criminal roaming around."

Nick snapped Sheriff Rivers a severe look. "I realize you can't take the responsibility for civilians investigating. I will though. I can't in good conscience leave her here alone. It's too dangerous."

Sheriff Rivers scratched his head. "I understand, especially after someone's already gone inside her cabin and broken her door. If he were to show up, depending on where we were…"

"Right, there's no one else here and we might not get back in time."

Emily shivered.

"Okay, let's go. Turn off your cell phones. We want to snoop not attract attention because one of us gets a call. We'll geo-locate in an emergency." Sheriff Rivers punched the shut-down button on his cell then Nick and Emily did the same. After Nick locked the office they walked to the forest, Sheriff Rivers on one side of Nick and Emily on the other.

Sheriff Rivers *tsked.* "I've lived here my entire life and used to play in these woods as a kid. I know them pretty well. I've never heard anyone refer to a spot as two bears."

Nick sent Sheriff Rivers a two-fingered salute. "So, it must be a code."

"Exactly. That makes our job more difficult." Stretching his back, Sheriff Rivers appeared an inch taller. "But we're up to the task." He stopped walking. "Why don't we sit for a bit and listen to the sounds in the forest."

Emily couldn't imagine what good the forest noises would do them, but Sheriff Rivers knew the area well, and he was the law enforcement officer in charge.

They perched on a fallen log. At first Emily heard nothing. Then the woods came alive with their own music—twigs snapped. Leves rustled. Rushing water swooshed in the distance. The forest seemed peaceful until screeching pierced the air. Emily jerked, peered above her, and trembled. "Look."

Nick gazed up. "A catamount."

"What's that?" Emily asked as she stared at the large cat-like creature walking over a boulder across from them.

Sheriff Rivers rubbed his hands over his knees. "That's the name people around here call any big cat.

Don't worry about him. If we need to handle him, we can. He'll probably leave soon though." Sheriff Rivers put his forefinger over his lips. "Listen, someone's talking." He turned his ear to the right.

Emily strained, but only heard the sounds of nature. In moments a person said something in a whisper. Or did they? She couldn't make it out. Maybe she was responding to the power of suggestion because Sheriff Rivers sat with a staid expression as though he took in every word.

Finally in a soft voice he said, "We need to walk to the right, but try not to make any noise. Stay behind me. We'll go single file."

Emily did exactly as he said. After she practically tip-toed thirty yards her breath hitched. She was in awe of how Sheriff Rivers picked up the sound of someone talking as soon as he did. They kept on the path for another three minutes before a man's voice filtered to them, his words flowing clearly in the quiet forest.

"Yes, I took care of Surley and Tough Guy, but I haven't found the flash drive. I couldn't follow the map."

Silence.

Emily put her hand over her mouth to hold in a gasp.

"I drew the line like you said. I put the words on it, but out here in the woods, it doesn't make sense. There's nothing in this forest that looks like two bears except two bears. Who thought up this stupid map?"

Silence.

"Well, if you understand it so well, you come to Sky High Campground, find it, and pay me."

Silence.

"I've already turned the place upside down. Maybe you gave me the wrong cabin number."

Emily jerked up her chin. It was the man who broke in her cabin. Having two strong men beside her gave her bold thoughts. She wanted Sheriff Rivers to follow the voice and arrest the man. She fired a sharp glance at him. He peered back and brought his index finger to his lips. His gesture didn't dampen her determination. She tilted her head in the direction of the voice. Sheriff Rivers gave her the shh sign again.

A few more seconds passed before Sherriff Rivers sliced a slow nod while Nick looked first at Sheriff Rivers then at Emily. He had one foot in front of the other like a lion ready to pounce on its prey.

Sheriff Rivers stood like a statue until finally he raised his arm and pulled it down as though signaling a calvary to charge. He darted toward the voice with Nick and Emily on his heels. The suspect took off running at lightning speed, Sheriff Rivers, Nick, and Emily ten feet behind him. All of a sudden, the suspect disappeared as though he evaporated into thin air.

Sheriff Rivers halted. Nick nearly ran into him while Emily bumped into Nick.

Sheriff Rivers turned around and looked at them as though he was in a fog. He shifted his gaze right then left. "That's impossible. He vanished."

Nick arched his eyebrows. "Oh yeah, he does that. He's disappeared twice on me. I chased him late at night. I told myself it was so dark I lost sight of him, but this…this is like he walked off the face of the earth in broad daylight."

Emily bit her lower lip. "Do you think there are tunnels underground connected to the holes?"

"Not likely. We would see entryways at the holes." Nick shook his head. "As to how he vanished, I don't get it."

Sheriff Rivers kicked away several twigs. "I think I know what he did."

"You do?" Emily asked, drawing out each word.

"We're all ears," Nick said.

"I've heard some of the city council folks talk about looking for a couple of underground caves as possible tourist attractions. So far, the proposal has only been mentioned in passing. I assume no one's interested in adding another attraction. We bring in more than enough people with the waterfalls, river sports, boating, and hiking."

Nick blinked. "What? Where are the caves?"

"That's a large part of the problem. We'd need to pay someone to find them. According to legend, over the years ridges of granite and underbrush have hidden them."

"Hmm. You think the rogue we're chasing is looking for them…" The muscles in Nick's jaw rippled. "…or found them?"

"I wouldn't rule that out. Someone involved is awfully familiar with these hills. He's either from around here or knows someone who is." Sheriff Rivers scrubbed his hand over his cheek. "At the moment no one comes to mind. I know most of the residents in the area. I can't imagine who he is." He let out an exasperated sigh. "I'm missing something. Not sure what though." He glanced at his watch. "I have to get back to Broken Arrow, but clearly we have more work to do."

They strode at a fast pace to the manager's office at

Sky High Campground, hurried inside, and sat down at Nick's desk.

"We'll touch base tomorrow. I'm determined to get to the bottom of this." Sheriff Rivers turned on his cell phone and it rang. "Rivers."

In moments after he answered he stiffened. "Thank you for telling us. Call me as soon as you know more details." A muscle twitched under his eye. "They found a dead body in the Crystal-Clear River in Blue Mountain—a man in his forties probably."

Nick rearranged papers in the inbox on his desk. "I can't say I'm surprised."

Emily placed her hands on her face. "That could've been me."

"We're going to take care of you. I know it's a lot, but trust us. We know more now than we did when you arrived. Believe me, we're taking it seriously. As for the police in Blue Mountain, they don't have a lot to share yet, but they said we had called about suspicious activity, so they want us to take caution, watch for anything unusual."

Emily blew out a big breath. "We've found plenty out of the ordinary already, but you can bet I'll be on the lookout for more."

Sheriff Rivers rubbed his hands over his knees and got up, his eyes soft in the corners. "We'll increase the patrol by your cabin at night."

"Thank you."

He turned toward Nick. "I'll phone you as soon as I know more, hopefully tomorrow."

Tomorrow? Emily hoped she'd see tomorrow.

Chapter Fourteen

Emily dipped a hot, chocolate chip cookie in milk. "Nothing better than dessert to soothe the soul."

"Yeah. I can't think of a place I'd rather be on a cold, Wednesday night than at your kitchen table." Nick held up a cookie. "I love these things. I haven't done this since high school."

Emily saw her opportunity to learn more about Nick. "So, you enlisted in the Army right after you graduated."

Sadness clouded Nick's eyes. "Yes."

"And then you decided to get out and go to college."

Nick winced. "Not exactly."

Emily stopped dipping her cookie and folded her hands, trying to calm the irritation building inside her. According to her friends and family, her expressions made her easy to read, so she suspected Nick could see how much she needed an answer.

"You're looking at me as though I'm trying to hide something. I'm not. I just don't talk about my military service."

Emily flinched. What on earth? Had he betrayed our country? After all, he was in military intelligence.

He slapped the table. "What? You think I'm a foreign spy or something. Believe me, my life's not that intriguing. I'm just an ordinary guy."

Nick was anything but ordinary.

"Look, if it means that much to you…" He shot her a narrow look.

She set her jaw firm to let him know if he wanted to continue the start of a relationship, he better tell her.

"I served four years and entered the selected reserve. That's how I'm paying for my education."

Emily bristled. Maybe Nick wanted to end this conversation, but she didn't. "And?"

"I hadn't planned to leave the military, but when I was in Afghanistan, something happened that threw my life out of kilter and put up a roadblock as far as serving."

"Would you mind explaining that? I couldn't be more confused."

"While I was overseas my fiancé died." Nick blurted it out as though he hated saying the words.

Emily broke eye contact with him. Should she give him a hug, or leave him alone? "How awful. I'm so sorry."

His cheeks drooped as though they were rubber and someone pulled them all the way down. "I wasn't any good for the military anymore. I just wanted to come home. By the end of my tour, to be perfectly honest with you, I was so distracted I was afraid I might mess up and cost some of my buddies their lives. As soon as my time was up, I got out and here I am."

Emily hugged Nick. Inside she cried for him. Getting dumped had sucked the life out of her. She understood his disconnect. Before she came to Sky

High, she built a shell as hard as the granite in these hills around her, letting nothing inside—not love, not anger, not joy.

First, fear of a man who might have tried to bury a body in her yard broke through the wall; then, Nick's kindness. He must've experienced the same type of defensiveness or worse. "How are you now? Do you miss serving?"

Nick looked down then up at Emily. "I like college more than I thought I would, so I'm convinced I made a good move, even though I sometimes feel out of place. I'm older than the other students. I've experienced things they haven't. I miss the military lifestyle, but at the same time, I believe eventually the intensity of war might have affected me, even if Caroline hadn't died." He swallowed hard. "Since I've opened up my baggage, I might as well tell you. I never intended to date again. I met Caroline when we were Freshmen in high school. We thought we'd stay together forever. I never would've left her to die alone." His voice cracked.

"I'm sure you wouldn't. You're much too conscientious to neglect someone you love." A kaleidoscope of emotions reeled inside Emily. She couldn't imagine what had been going on between her and Nick, but obviously she had misread his intentions, but his kiss…"

He stood, pulled her up and hugged her so tight she could barely breathe before he stepped back, caressed her cheek, and put his lips to hers in a long kiss.

Emily swam in an aura of confusion. Conflicting thoughts exploded like firecrackers in her brain. Nick just professed his love for Caroline, but he acted as though he cared for her. She melted in his arms just as she had the first time he kissed her.

He released his hold. "I think that explains my current situation."

Emily was speechless, her judgement at a standstill. She had been on an emotional merry-go-round. Suddenly it stopped turning, leaving her atop a static pony.

Nick must have seen her confusion because he pulled her close to him. "I'm sorry. Let me put that another way. Once when my mother took my brother's side in a fight, I told her she loved him, but didn't love me. She said, "Oh no. It's not like that. Love isn't like tea in a pitcher. Love never runs out. There's plenty of it to go around for everyone."

Though she tried to put Nick's words in perspective, they bounced off of her like tennis balls. Obviously, he didn't want to talk about Caroline, and clearly, she impacted his life in a profound way, so how…how…could the two of them have a future? It wasn't like Donnie. After she got to know Nick, Donnie became a bad memory, but Nick's love for Caroline would live forever. She pushed away the tears forming inside her and nearly choked, but she refused to cry.

She rubbed her temples to get rid of the ache in them. At least she could feel something, even if it was pain. More upset over the possibility of losing Nick than she ever imagined she would be, she tried to understand what he meant for her to hear. Was he saying his love for Caroline was too strong for him to get involved with anyone else? Was he telling her he had a little love left in him even after Caroline died and took most of it with her?

As if sensing the questions swirling in her head,

Nick pulled her into his arms. "Only since I met you, I've realized even though Caroline will remain precious to me, it's like my mother said, I have more love to give. It's odd. I wondered if in time I could care about anyone else, but now I know I can. I have a friend who's a firm believer in love at first sight." He scrunched his shoulders. "I'm not saying that's what happened, but I realized as soon as I spent a little time with you, I didn't want to let you go without getting to know you better."

Emily's blood pressure started to go down. "So, you're saying you think there could be something between us, you and me, even though…"

"Yeah, most definitely."

Emily saw the merry-go-around moving in the distance. She smiled when the dormant pony started to go up and down to the music.

Nick released her. "What about the jerk that left you at the altar?" Nick tapped Emily's temple. "Is he still in there?"

Nick's touch brought Emily back to the moment, but it seemed surreal. How could two broken-hearted souls not only cross paths under this most unusual circumstance, but also share a mutual admiration? "Donnie still inside my head? Absolutely not. I've realized who he is and thank goodness, the Lord stepped in at the last minute. I mean maybe Donnie and I were wrong for each other. Giving Donnie the benefit of a doubt, perhaps he realized it. Even so, he could've picked a better way of handling the situation."

Nick laughed. "Nah. Donnie's a few mountain apples short of a full basket, if you ask me. It's his loss. Let's have our cookies and milk then figure out how we're going to catch this escape artist."

"Yeah." Emily dipped her cookie in her milk.

Nick took a bite of his. "So back to the guy looking for the flash drive. Surely, he won't return after he told the person he talked to on the phone he might have gotten the wrong cabin number." He squeezed her hand. "But don't worry. We won't take any chances. I wrote down the names of several movies we can watch until the wee hours of the morning."

"Ah, that's not necessary. You need your sleep. After all, you're staying next door now."

"That's true, but let's finish eating, turn on the TV, and see how it goes."

"Okay."

They finished the milk and cookies, and Nick found a film. Before he turned up the volume, he said, "I'm going to the woods tomorrow and find that underground cave. The whole time Sheriff Rivers was talking about it, I kept telling myself, 'No wonder I thought I was losing that scoundrel.' I'm going to the area where we were and search every inch of it."

"Me too."

"You might not want to come along this time. Once I find this guy, it's not going to be a pretty sight."

"All the more reason why I should go to keep you from doing something foolish."

Nick laughed. "No. No. No."

Emily scooted a foot away from Nick. "Either I'll go with you, or I'll go alone, but this man has harassed me enough."

Nick studied her for several moments. "You're serious."

Emily sent Nick an intense stare. "Absolutely."

Nick sighed. "You win."

Emily slid over next to him. He turned up the volume and put his arm on the back of the sofa. His chin headed for his chest several times. He jerked it up and stared at the television, but finally he dozed. When the movie ended, Emily nudged him. "Hey sleepyhead, the movie's over. I insist you go home and get some sleep."

"You're right. I need to start tomorrow refreshed. I have to catch up on paperwork." He stood. "Promise to call if anything out of the ordinary happens." He gave her a peck on the cheek and left.

~

Sleeping until nearly noon the next day, when Emily awoke, she sat on the side of the bed and rubbed her brow. She would leave Nick in peace to complete his tasks unless, of course, she had an emergency. She doubted she would. Even though most burglaries occurred during the day because no one was home, so far, this lowlife appeared to prefer breaking into her cabin at night. She would sit on the porch and relax for a change.

She prepared an omelet with bacon bits, onions, and cheese. After she finished eating and cleaned the kitchen, she sat in a rocker overlooking the landscape to carry out her plan, but she didn't relax. While she gazed at the landscape and watched a squirrel munching something he probably had buried during the fall, in her mind she saw images of a man with long hair slinking around her cabin like the snake he was. She got up and paced back and forth. Biting her nail, she couldn't stay still for wanting to end the harassment. She'd snooped before to get information for articles she wrote and had never gotten caught by a criminal. She wrung her hands and walked around the yard. By twilight she'd decided to go out and find evidence to give Sheriff Rivers for an arrest warrant.

At night's first breath, she put on her heavy coat and gloves, grabbed her flashlight and left. Determined to find the proof she needed, she walked in blackness with only the glow from the flashlight, dim moonlight, and stars to illuminate the way. She stopped to listen for friendly sounds to tell her there were no catamounts, or other dangerous animals close by. She didn't hear any sticks breaking. She turned her ear upward. Not even an elk's sharp hooves hitting granite interrupted the silence. Most of the creatures, except for a couple of raccoons and a possum scooting past her, must've been asleep.

A stick cracked and every muscle in her body tightened. If the animals weren't making noise, it was him. She had to carry through and get the information she needed, but she had no idea she'd be this scared. She switched off the flashlight and stood trembling. A closer crunch resounded. Leaves rustled. Twigs broke.

More footfalls. She rubbed beads of sweat from her upper lip. A spooky figure moved in the moonglow and disappeared into the shadows. Coming toward her? She looked into nature's black abyss and went limp inside. She had to move. Get out of his way.

She stepped back, tripped, and fell on underbrush. Trying to crawl beneath it and hide, she'd barely begun to stir the foliage when she dropped into a hole. Landing on a mound of soft dirt in a pitch-black pit, she gulped down breaths to keep from screaming. Trying to adjust to the lack of light she blinked over and over.

She sat still, listening for what seemed like hours without hearing a sound. With a shaky finger, she switched on the flashlight. A rat crawled on a ledge across form her. The acid in her stomach turned sour and she gagged. She focused the light overhead and beams bounced off of white stalactites. Shining the flashlight toward her feet, she cringed. Stalagmites. Thank goodness, she landed beside one of those and not on it. She gasped. One of the caves Sheriff Rivers had mentioned.

This discovery is important.

She tried to concentrate on gathering information, but it took all of her stamina to watch the squeaking rodent. She'd make sure she moved if he headed her way. Finally, he went in the other direction. She stood, swinging the flashlight all around the cave. The beams illuminated a metal box, possibly steel, about three feet wide and one foot long at the other end of the cave.

Should she open it? The underbrush above rustled. She jumped, switched off the flashlight, and ducked into an opening. The washed-out area the size of a closet closed in on her. She could barely breathe.

Light seeped into the cave. A man entered carrying a flashlight. Her heart pounded.

His feet hit the floor with a thud. He hunched over. Then sprang upright with his back to her. "Come here, Little Roy."

The rat reappeared. He gave it a small piece of an apple. The rodent squeaked excitedly. The man chuckled and rubbed its noggin.

Ewww. Emily's skin crawled as the man reached out his hand and fed it another bite. Didn't he know rats could carry disease, like bubonic plague. At last, he finished feeding and petting the rat and walked out of her sight.

She sat with her knees pulled up against her chest and tried to think. She had to calm down and get out of here. Her insides raced like a runaway car, her mind, quiet as a rock. She was trapped. Tears cascaded down her cheeks.

The man paced around the cave, walking past the washed-out space. Squinting, she got a better look at him. His bushy hair covered most of his face. She tried to scrunch up more. If only she could become a stalagmite.

The rat squeaked again.

"What is it, Little Roy? Are you still hungry?"

Squeak, squeak.

"You really want me to go get another apple peeling?"

Squeak, squeak.

"All right. What kind of man would I be if I let such a cute little creature starve?"

Emily swallowed hard to keep from throwing up.

The shadowy figure shone his flashlight onto the entryway and pulled himself up by clutching a strong tree root. When his feet disappeared, Emily turned on her flashlight. Taking tentative steps, she came out of hiding. The rat stared at her with beady eyes. She pocketed the flashlight and took hold of the tree root. Footfalls near the mouth of the cave drifted away. She pulled herself out. Then she ran away as fast as she could. She didn't know where she was going, just away from the cave, beyond the danger. When she could run no farther, she collapsed onto the ground.

Chapter Fifteen

Nick woke early, the sun shining through the blinds in his bedroom making stripes across the light blue and green comforter. He threw back the covers, sprang up, and pulled on a pair of jeans and a sweater.

Hopefully, Emily was already up. He didn't like the idea of dragging her with him into the woods to search for a cavern that might or might not house a murderer. At the same time, having her look for it alone concerned him more. She might slow him down a bit, but he wouldn't let anything happen to her. He grabbed his coat, locked the door, and strode to her cabin.

He knocked for five minutes. Why didn't she answer? Had she called him for help in the middle of the night? Surely, he hadn't slept through the phone ringing again. He pounded louder this time and got no answer. All right, he was going in.

He pulled his universal key from his pants pocket and entered. All seemed quiet. She must still be asleep. Good. He'd explain later he went ahead because he didn't want to wake her. As he turned to leave, he bumped into the hall tree. Her down jacket wasn't there. He steadied the stand and froze debating whether or not to look in the rear of the house.

The last thing he wanted to do was disturb her, invade her privacy, or worse yet scare her, but he had to know she was okay. He peeked into the bedroom.

The bed was unmade. He listened for water running in the bathroom. Nothing. With every hair on his arms standing on end, he raced outside and locked the door. Leaning against the wall to think, he wiped his sweaty brow.

He hadn't planned to go to the office today because he wanted to hunt for the caves. Maybe Emily was there. He ran to the rustic building. No Emily.

He had to confront scenarios he didn't even want to imagine. Maybe Emily ventured into the woods on her own, or worse. Maybe someone forced her into leaving the cabin. He dashed into the forest calling her name. Fear of losing her ran through his veins like a rushing river and nearly knocked him to the ground. He'd already lost Caroline. Not Emily too. They hadn't had a chance to get to know one another.

He halted to catch his breath. Heartache brought him to his knees. No. This couldn't happen. Did that ruthless degenerate have Emily? Was she in the forest tied up or unconscious? He sprang up and charged ahead, trying to look carefully at the landscape. "Emily. Emily. Emily." He hollered so loud his voice grew hoarse.

~

Emily didn't have the strength to push her body off of the ground, but she'd never wanted to get out of anywhere as much as she wanted out of this forest. Thank goodness, the sun was up. The MO of the criminal creating havoc in these hills told her he usually stayed away from her cabin in broad daylight. They had seen him roaming the woods during the day though. If she could only get up, she'd go home, take a shower, and go to sleep. She thought she heard her name, but who would call her out here in this wilderness?

She strained to listen. Someone said her name again, or she was hearing things. Surely, she didn't imagine her name wafting through the barren woods. No. It had to be Nick. She pushed up and yelled, "Yes."

She heard her name again this time with footsteps in the distance. The sound of Nick's voice gave her the strength to sit up. "Yes. Yes."

"Emily."

"I'm over here."

The footfalls grew closer. Her name louder.

She tried to stand, but someone pulled her up from behind and turned her around. "Nick, I'm so glad to see you."

"You're as white as snow."

"You are too."

"Where have you been?" The tone of his voice left no doubt he was miffed.

"I told you I was going to find the cave, and I did."

Nick's eyelids popped wide open.

"I forgot my phone. I thought I had it in my coat pocket, but now I remember, it's in my purse. I couldn't get a picture or video, but I saw him. I hate it. I just hate it. I couldn't see his features because he has bushy hair that covers most of his face. Well, that and the dark. Oh Nick, it was so dark. You wouldn't believe how black it was all around me. But, but I had brought my flashlight. Wouldn't forget that. I shined it in the cave. That was before he showed up. Yes, before. And there was a rat crawling on a ledge. And Nick, you won't believe it. He came in with a piece of an apple peeling, not the rat. He was already there—the man. He fed the rat then he petted it. Eww." Emily shivered with the thought. "It was awful. It's just not normal."

"You're right. Something's up. Let's sit down." Nick guided Emily to a log, where they sat side by side then he took her hand in his. "Go on."

"Well, there isn't much more. The rat kept squeaking. I think the man thought it wanted more to eat, so he left. That's when I came out of the alcove, the place I was hiding. It was a blessing it was there, but it was tiny, no bigger than a closet, and I could hardly breathe. I was so scared. When I walked back into the main area of the cave, the rat stared at me. Gave me the creeps."

Nick put his arm around her shoulder. "Everything's fine now. How did you get out of there."

"I grabbed hold of the tree root and pulled myself up. I saw him, the man, do that, so I did it too. Once I escaped, I fled as hard and fast as I could. I didn't know where I was headed, but when I saw the sun, I figured he wouldn't come after me in the daylight. Too risky." Emily almost forgot to add the important evidence. "There was a metal container, probably steel, about three feet in width and one foot in length at the other end of the cave. I was going to open it, but he entered the cave before I had the chance." She twisted a button on her coat. "He was inches away from me. Only by the grace of God did I survive."

"Take it from a military guy, don't ever open anything if you don't know what's in it. You're right. Divine intervention may have saved you. From what, we may never know, but that's not the point." Nick set his jaw. "I *will* confiscate that box in due time."

Emily rubbed her cheeks. "What a mess."

Nick pulled her next to him and held her tight, his touch sending strength through her. "How about you go home and get a shower while I find us something to eat? Then, if you are up to it, I'll call Sheriff Rivers, tell him about the cave. At a minimum this rat-feeder is a trespasser."

Emily sighed. "I hope I'll remember where it was. It was so dark. I was so frightened."

"We'll worry about that later. Right now, we need to get you to the cabin."

Within thirty minutes Emily sat on the sofa in a pair of jeans and a T-shirt beside Nick, who hovered over her like a mother bird.

"Are you sure you're alright?"

"Absolutely." Emily raked her hand through her long hair, still damp from her shower. "I'm a little tired, but ready to capture the man in the cave."

"Okay, I'll get Sheriff Rivers over here." Nick drummed his fingers on his knee. "The way we studied the forest, I can't believe none of us spotted the entrance. I specifically looked at the underbrush and nothing seemed out of the ordinary."

"I guess you have to fall in it." Emily chuckled, and Nick laughed.

He patted her back. "Well, we know it's there now."

"Even so." Emily placed her hand on her chest. "I should've tried to see landmarks even if it was dark." She snapped her fingers. "Every once in a while, I noticed a faint glow from the moon or stars on a tree or rock. I'll probably recognize the entrance to the cave if I see it again."

"Don't worry. We'll find it."

Emily glanced at her watch. "Do you think Sheriff Rivers is in his office yet?"

Nick pulled his cell phone out of his pocket and punched the numbers. "Good morning, this is Nick at the campground."

Silence.

"Emily accidentally fell into one of the caves you mentioned and barely escaped. There was a guy either living there or using it as a hideout."

Silence.

"What?"

Silence.

"Yes. It was dark, but she can find it."

Silence.

"Thanks."

Nick hung up and turned to Emily. "He's coming at one o'clock. I'm going to the office until then. Why don't you take a nap and meet us there."

"I will."

Nick kissed her on the forehead.

Nice.

"I'll see you then." He got up and left.

If only she could find the spot where she fell into the cave.

Chapter Sixteen

Emily entered the manager's office while Sheriff Rivers held the door for her.

He smiled and said, "Hey," the word accompanied by a jolly chuckle.

Emily took lighter steps as his greeting put her at ease around him. "Hi."

"I hear you found a huge lead for us." His eyes sparkled.

Emily sensed a twinge of acceptance in his tone. Was he finally warming up to her as a suitable tag along with him and Nick? "I hope so."

Nick rose from his desk chair and directed his gaze to Sheriff Rivers. "I think you had something to tell us too."

"I sure do. I asked the police in Blue Mountain to send the deceased's DNA to a lab using the fast forensic test for DNA. We have results already."

Nick rubbed his hands together. "That's great. Tell us who he was."

Emily braced herself. Better to finally know.

"Surley Johnson. He grew up in Broken Arrow and left right after high school. He had been arrested for petty crimes in Atlanta, Washington, D.C., and New

York. No felonies, especially not assaults or murders. They found his phone on the riverbank several miles from the body. The last person he called was Tough Guy Roggue, which doesn't tell us much. That's an alias if I ever heard one."

Nick blinked. "Uh, I wonder if the man who was in the cave is Tough Guy Roggue."

Sheriff Rivers motioned toward the door and looked at Nick. "Let's find out who he is." He tilted his head toward Emily. "You're still responsible for our guide, right?"

"You bet."

Emily sighed as they left. She understood the sheriff couldn't recruit citizens to solve murders. At the same time, this was more like a search party. He seemed happy about her find. She'd give him the benefit of a doubt. After all that had happened, he probably *was* concerned about putting her in danger.

They walked into the woods underneath a sunny sky, a sparrow flitting above them. Emily wished she could be as free as the bird. At least she didn't have to try to locate the cave in rain, ice, or snow. "I'm sorry I can't tell you exactly where I was. I can say look for a lot of underbrush clumped together. The foliage appears rooted, but I think it was designed using synthetic plants, or he replenished them every so often." Emily put her forefinger to her cheek. "When I think of it, there are more large bushes there than in other places."

Nick gave her a thumbs up. "That's a big help."

"Got it." Sheriff Rivers took his time surveying their surroundings, examining every leaf and twig. "We won't move forward until we cover each space thoroughly."

They walked to another area, and Nick halted.

"What?" Sheriff Rivers asked.

"We could go to the spot where I found Emily and start searching from there."

"Good idea."

Emily strode on one side of Nick, Sheriff Rivers on the other.

Nick looked toward Sheriff Rivers. "After I chased him into the forest once, I couldn't believe he came back and tried to get in the cabin again. He had to know I watched it."

"He's crazy." Emily chimed in.

"He could prove even more dangerous than we first thought. He's been pretty lucky trespassing, possibly hiding other breaches of law also." Sheriff Rivers tightened his facial muscles. "We're going to change that."

"Check this out." Nick stopped and pointed at the ground. "Some of this brown grass and these weeds are smashed. He could've walked in this area. Let's fan out. One of us to the right, one dead center, and one to the left."

Sheriff Rivers stepped back. "Are you sure?"

"Yes." Nick held up his cell. "We've got these."

Emily nodded. Sheriff Rivers was probably still uneasy about having her along. She appreciated his position and how conscientious he was. He didn't understand though. She had a lot at stake in this investigation—saving her life *and* the story for "Blue Mountain News." Not only that, she *was* a responsible person. "I'll take the middle because I probably ran in a straight line, or at least close to one."

"Just observe. Do not engage or enter any cave

under any circumstances." Sheriff Rivers' voice held authority.

"Don't worry. If I find anything, I'm calling one of you."

Sheriff Rivers gave Emily a thumbs up. "Exactly, that's what we all should do. Step away from the cave, find cover, and alert the others. No one make a move until we're all together. One last time, are we all in agreement?"

"Yes," Nick said.

Emily echoed him. She couldn't wait to put a stop to Tough Guy Roggue, or whoever he was.

"Don't leave a pebble unturned. I could bring in the man Emily saw in the cave as a person of interest by nightfall if we're all diligent."

After they fanned out Emily walked alone with a chill running up her spine. The fear from her excursion into the home of the killer had stayed with her. She'd never share her anxiety with Nick or Sheriff Rivers though. She would not let them, or herself down. With the images of the excessive underbrush and the tree root she had seen at the cave etched in her mind, she would find that exact hidden cavern.

She scrutinized broken sticks, rocks, and pieces of leaves as she walked, hoping to see something familiar. As she kicked a broken branch out of her path she heard swishing. She flinched as a squirrel scampered away. "Whew. I'm sorry I disturbed you, little fellow."

Above her a northern bluebird tweeted making the woods seem like a friendly place. If only that were true. Wickedness lurked underground below the mirage of peace. Why did nothing appear out of the ordinary? To do her part, she had wanted to locate the cave, but since she hadn't, she hoped Nick or Sheriff Rivers had had better luck. Water roared in the distance. She never made it to the cascade last night. If she reached the waterfall she'd gone too far.

She spotted underbrush all clumped together. That had to be the place. She charged toward it and yanked on a limb, but it didn't budge. She squatted and examined it. She was certain this was the location of the cave, but all of the bushes were solidly rooted.

Her mistake weighed on her. Should she stay on this path? A strong voice inside urged her to continue in the same direction. She trudged farther into the woods, looking carefully every foot or so, inspecting each inch of earth, daring the dirt to withhold the answer she sought.

Her neck hurt from looking down for what seemed like hours. She stretched and leaned her head back toward the sky. Transitioning her gaze back to the ground she saw the right place. Yes. This was it. It had to be. Once again, she got on her hands and knees and analyzed the foliage only to see it was rooted.

The sun hung low, and the sky turned gray. She pulled her cell phone out of her pocket and checked it. Nope. She hadn't missed a call. Neither Sheriff Rivers nor Nick had found the cave, and she knew why. It was on her path. She would not rest easy until she located it. Her legs ached. She wanted to sit down but forced her muscles to push forward. It was nearly dark. She had not succeeded, but she would not give up. She would find the cave before she left these woods. Her cell phone rang. "Hi Nick."

"We're going to call it a day and start again in the morning."

"No. I know it's out here. We can't stop now."

"Emily. Listen to me. There's no reason to repeat last night. Get back right now, please."

"All right. If you'll let me stay on this path tomorrow, I know I can find it."

"Agreed. See you soon."

Nick was right. Since the sun shone bright when they left, she hadn't even brought a flashlight. As much as she hated to accept defeat, she started walking toward the spot where she left Nick and Sheriff Rivers.

She covered only twenty feet before she heard footfalls behind her.

An elk?

She ducked behind a boulder, just in case. Whoever or whatever would pass soon. She waited to hear the footpads fade into the distance. Silence fell. Maybe an elk smelled her. She should contact Nick. No. What if it was the man from the cave? He would hear keystroke motions for a text.

She muted her phone. Willed her body motionless. She looked left. Right. No way to escape. Only a ghostly aura on the trees.

Squeak. Squeak. Squeak.

Emily went weak. Get away from them. She jerked her head to the right. Nothing. She looked behind her. Another rock.

Squeak. Squeak. Squeak.

She trembled. *Lord, please help me.*

A twig broke. Emily saw nothing. That was it. If she couldn't see anything neither could he. She got on her hands and knees and crept into a shadow. A streak of light fell over the space between her and the underbrush.

Squeak. Squeak. Squeak.

Shut up, rat. The rat stopped as though it read her mind. More twigs snapped. A man's silhouette appeared. She crouched in the shadow, watching, waiting. His hair swished from side to side.

She moved into another shadow farther away. The footsteps fell nearby. Frozen like a statue, she cut her eyes left and right. Another boulder lay in front of her. But wait. The moon shined on it. She couldn't go there. She spotted a hollow oak tree. If she could get inside, he'd never find her. The moon and stars lit a wide stripe of earth between her and the oak tree. Nooo. Her head started to ache. The steps came closer. If she crossed in the light, he would see her.

Oh Lord, please help me.

A shadow moved across the patch of light.

Thank you, Lord.

She crawled as fast as her hands and knees would take her. She tried to squeeze into the hollow of the tree. Nope. Ah. She scooted behind its large trunk.

Dead leaves crunched as he paced nearby.

Squeak. Squeak.

She scrunched her knees to her ribcage, pulled her arms tight around them. Her silent scream pounded in her ears. Sticks cracked. She muffled a gasp. He stopped in front of her with his back toward her. The rat was on his shoulder, his beady eyes looking at her.

Squeak. Squeak. Squeak. The rat squeaked over and over, faster and faster.

Shut up rat. She held her breath.

Someone else pounded the ground. Who made the thuds? His partner? Flashlight beams shone on either side of the tree. She inched a peek.

Nick and Sheriff Rivers came toward her.

Footpads going away. They grew faint. The squeaking faded into the distance and disappeared.

She should follow him. At least, get up and see where he went. After all, that's why she came to the woods tonight.

Nick and Sheriff Rivers walked five feet from her. *No. Help. Don't go away.* She stood. "Over here. I'm over here." She spoke in a near whisper.

Nick turned, grabbed her, and hugged her.

"Thank God, you're alright," Sheriff Rivers said.

Nick released his hold. "What happened?"

Emily sputtered as she reviewed her steps. "He was here. I, I don't know when or where he first saw me. I…" She gulped for air. "I was coming to meet you two until I heard someone. Then the rat squeaked. That rat. I guess, in a way, it was good for me he had the nasty thing. Its squeak alerted me. I kept moving…" Emily sucked in a deep breath. "…moving in the shadows from one dark place to another until I got behind the hollowed-out tree. I knew…I knew I should follow him to find the cave, but I couldn't. I don't know what happened. It was like I was glued to the ground."

Sheriff Rivers nodded. "Yes, ma'am, that's understandable. You should not have trailed him. We want to catch him not lose you." He stepped back. "We shouldn't have allowed you to come out here, but I don't think…"

"You couldn't have stopped me. Anyway, it's obvious. I was better off with the two of you than alone. Lesson learned. I see that now. I will never walk in these woods by myself again."

Nick glimpsed the Heavens. "Thank goodness, for

that."

Sheriff Rivers turned away from the forest. "I believe we've done all we can for tonight. I'll come back tomorrow, bring him in as a person of interest in the murder, and book him for trespassing. I'll do everything in my power to get to the bottom of this case. You can sleep on it, count on it, and know it will happen. He's caused all the trouble he's going to. I'll work almost around the clock, seven days a week until he's looking at me through my jailhouse bars."

Emily blew out a big breath. "Thank you." She wasn't sure how much Sheriff Rivers could accomplish, but his determination sparked her optimism.

Chapter Seventeen

Sunday morning Emily walked to the Sky High Campground chapel. Even though there was no service, sitting in the rustic wooden sanctuary, she cherished the quiet. Peering out the floor to ceiling glass windows, she soaked in the majesty of the hills. Then she sat for a while with peace wrapped around.

Later that afternoon she took lighter steps to meet Sheriff Rivers and Nick in the manager's office.

They stood at Nick's desk. "I can't believe this guy's right under our noses, and we can't catch him," Nick said.

Sheriff Rivers clenched his fists. "We're going to find that cave today. Emily must've gotten close to it yesterday, or he wouldn't have seen her."

"Good morning."

Nick and Sheriff Rivers directed their attention to Emily.

"Hi, there, I was just discussing your encounter yesterday. Today, we'll study every inch of ground on the path you took. Tonight the man harassing you will sleep in my jail."

"If we accomplish our goal," Nick added.

Emily shifted her weight from one foot to the other.

"I noticed several landmarks, so I can show you where I went and point out two clumps of rooted underbrush."

"Let's go," Nick said.

Outside, Emily charged ahead. In addition to finding the hideout, she wanted to locate the dead body. No one had even mentioned the corpse in the past few days. Nick and Sheriff Rivers would see eventually. For now, their agenda was to search for the man with that disgusting rat. Personally, she would breathe easier after they caught that cave-dwelling, rat-feeding ne'er do well. He was the one stalking her. Her instincts told her there was a connection between him and the killer, a strong one—like they were the same person.

The air, a little colder than usual, chilled her to the bone and she yearned for the warmth of her cabin. She couldn't relax knowing the intruder still roamed around freely though. She approached a cluster of underbrush. "These look like the fake shrubs, but they aren't." She placed her hands on her hips. "When I pulled at these plants yesterday, I found them firmly planted in the ground."

Sheriff Rivers nodded. "It's an advantage to know what not to investigate. Saves us time."

"There are more bushes resembling these a little farther up. They aren't the right ones either. I do think the cave's close to here though."

"Thanks to you, we know it's out here. We'll get him today." Resolve resounded in Sheriff Rivers' voice. He led the way with Nick and Emily following. Stopping in front of the next group of underbrush, he turned to face Emily. "I assume this is the second group of shrubbery you mentioned."

"Right."

"We're close. I can feel it," Nick said.

Sheriff Rivers started hiking, picking up his pace. Twenty minutes later Emily spotted the entrance to the cave. She stopped and pointed. "There it is," she whispered, recalling all that had happened there.

Sheriff Rivers darted to the cave and hollered, "Come out. I know you're in there."

Silence.

Sheriff Rivers started uncovering the faux entryway. Leaves flew through the air as sticks and entire plants shot toward the sky until finally the opening appeared in full view. He stared at the cavity. "Come out. You're under arrest for trespassing and breaking and entering."

Silence.

Sheriff Rivers grabbed hold of the tree root and slid down, followed by Nick.

Emily glared at the root and hesitated. She clutched her throat as the memory of staying in the cave horrified her. The box inside was vital to this case. She had to direct Nick and Sheriff Rivers to it. She swallowed her fear, grasped the root, and went inside. A musty, earthy smell and darkness greeted her.

Sheriff Rivers shined around a flashlight. "There's nothing here. Are you sure we're in the right place?"

Emily's stomach knotted like some of the tree roots in these hills. She could never forget this cave. "I fell on this spot." She leaned over several stalagmites and studied them. "Yes, right beside these." She charged to the washed-out area. "This is where I hid nearly all night long." She took erratic breaths recalling how afraid she was. "Look. It's about the size of a closet. Go over there and see for yourselves." She twirled around scanning the cave. "Where is he? And where's that rat?"

Nick strode over and peered at the area where Emily had hidden. "Yeah. I see it's close quarters, but thank goodness, it is here."

"I hadn't thought of my temporary prison as a blessing, but you're right. It was."

Emily peered at the ceiling, "Those are the stalactites I saw."

"It's definitely a cave," Sheriff Rivers said.

Emily sighed. He didn't believe it was "the" cave. "I'm in the right place. There was a metal receptacle at the other end. It was about three feet wide and one foot long. I think it was steel."

"I don't doubt you, but he's not here. The container isn't either. Unfortunately, we can't do anything except look for clues that might head us in the right direction."

Emily turned away from Sheriff Rivers and Nick to hide her frustration. "I can't believe this."

Nick placed his hand on her shoulder, and she faced him.

"It's okay," he said.

Sheriff Rivers walked toward the spot where she had seen the steel container. Nick stepped into the washed-out area, and she propped herself against the cave's wall.

Nick returned, the lines of his face tightened, his eyes firm as he paced back and forth examining the ground. In several minutes he bent over then straightened. "Ah, ha, see what I found."

"What?" Emily didn't even look.

"Your pen."

Emily snapped her gaze toward him.

He held up his find with a handkerchief around the part he clutched.

Emily put her hand in her jacket pocket. "It must've fallen out when I crawled from here. I need to be more careful. I wouldn't make a very good undercover cop."

Nick put his arm around her shoulder. "You're making a fine one, but with more hard work and a bit of luck you can return to tourist status soon."

Sheriff Rivers joined them. "It appears the receptacle made an imprint on the ground down there. Apparently, he's moved on though."

Emily rocked back on her heels. Thank goodness Sheriff Rivers found verification. "At least the rat's not here."

Sheriff Rivers walked over to Nick. "What have you got there?"

Nick handed the pen to him.

"Blue Mountain News? Why would that be here?"

Nick motioned toward Emily. "She's a crime reporter for the newspaper in Blue Mountain."

"Hmm. Interesting." He studied the exposed part of the pen closer. "Why didn't the guy take it with him?"

"Maybe he didn't notice it. Even if he did, this man's so brazen, so arrogant he probably didn't think we'd search this place."

Emily nodded then curled a strand of her hair around her finger. "So, what now?"

"All isn't lost simply because he isn't here. There are quite a few footprints in the back of the cave. CSI can get impressions of those and dust for fingerprints. It would be easier if they could get the prints off of the pen. Unfortunately, if he didn't notice it, he didn't touch it."

"He was busy with that nasty rat."

"As sure as I'm the sheriff, we'll lift prints from somewhere in here."

Was Sheriff Rivers trying to convince her and Nick or himself there were fingerprints? *Think Emily. What did he touch?* "He had to use the tree root to go in and out."

"That's a great suggestion if we didn't contaminate it when we entered."

Emily's enthusiasm sank like a rock in one of these mountain lakes. Had she endured the harrowing ordeal in the cave for nothing? She surveyed the area. "Oh. I know. There." She pointed to the place where the rat had been. "Don't anybody touch that ledge. He stayed over there talking to the rat, petting the filthy thing, and feeding it."

Sheriff Rivers' eyes danced.

Satisfaction swelled in Emily's chest.

"Thank you. I'll inform CSI as soon as they arrive." Sheriff Rivers brushed off his hands.

"Will someone work on Sunday to make the impressions and…" Emily looked at Nick. "And lift any fingerprints?"

Sheriff Rivers chuckled. "There's someone available at the sheriff's office 24 / 7. Unfortunately, criminals don't work nine to five weekdays."

"Of course, I don't know what I was thinking."

"Don't you worry. We're on it now. I hate you fell in this cave. I would never want you to investigate on your own. I certainly don't want you in danger." Sheriff Rivers' voice trailed off. "I've been trying to avoid endangering you, but…"

Emily laughed. "I won't hear of it."

"Don't ever investigate alone." Sheriff Rivers emphasized each word.

Emily never wanted to go through anything so frightening again. She nodded. "Don't worry. I learned my lesson, shaking, scared out of my wits in that washed out space."

"We do have a place to start thanks to you."

Wow. A thank you from Sheriff Rivers. "You're welcome." Had he accepted her as a suitable sidekick? Time would tell. His acknowledgement encouraged Emily, but so far, they had no real evidence, no idea where to find this creep. Not only that, Sheriff Rivers still didn't mention the dead body she saw. She'd ask Nick for an update when they returned to the cabin.

Chapter Eighteen

Nick sat on the sofa and pulled Emily close to him. "I know it's hard to think about anything except the case, but we should try. Sheriff Rivers is on this cave man Houdini. We're making progress." He gazed toward the fireplace. "I'll start a fire, and we can relax in front of it."

"Good idea. There are still a lot of logs on the back porch."

"I know. I chopped the wood before you arrived." Nick stood and winked at Emily. "Why don't you make some of your famous herbal coffee blend while I get a blaze going."

Emily sprang up. "You got it."

In no time the aroma of Emily's hazelnut brew mixed with the smell of oak burning in the crackling fire. She set their cups on the coffee table then sank into the sofa. "Ahh, earlier when I was cold, I yearned for the warmth of my cabin. I'm going to sit here for a minute and bask in the peace."

Nick joined her and put his arm around her shoulder. "Bask all you want. I'll make sure no one disturbs us."

Emily picked up her drink, took a sip, and gazed at the flames as though the blaze mesmerized her.

The fire popping created coziness. When Nick destressed after a difficult day in the military, he referred to his relaxed state as his comfort zone. In college the gauge described his status at the end of each semester after he completed finals. In the past he had found the job here lowkey and hadn't needed to drift from being tied in knots. Not this time though. With the dangerous man roaming the hills at Sky High, he had faced pressure every day. At last, with Sheriff Rivers on the job and Emily by his side, he slipped into his comfort zone.

At twilight, a thud and scraping noise jarred him.

Emily shot up while he bounded off of the sofa and charged out the door with his blood running hot to capture the man with the rat. Outdoors, he stopped, turned toward Emily standing beside him, and shrugged. "I don't get it. There's no one out here."

Emily looked left then right. "Where did he go?" She snapped her fingers. "He must've moved to a hiding place so close to this cabin he got to it before you saw him." She pointed toward the sliding glass doors. "I can't believe I got so relaxed I forgot to close the curtains."

Nick swallowed hard. How could he have been so careless? "My mistake. I'm supposed to know how to protect myself and others."

Emily patted his back. "That's all right. Don't sell yourself short. We're both exhausted."

"I bet he was waiting outside for an opportunity to break into the cabin, probably would have if we hadn't been here."

"Just thinking about that man getting in the cabin again makes my skin crawl." Emily rubbed her arms. "He's so creepy along with whatever else he is."

Nick made a fist with his right hand and hit the wall. It hurt, but not as much as his pride. "I have to do better."

Emily hugged him. "That's impossible. No one can work twenty-four hours a day." She smiled. "Maybe that's an exaggeration, but not by much." She lightly punched his biceps. "The way he disappears into thin air, I wonder if he's part ghost."

Nick laughed. "That's it." He held up his hand in rebuttal. "No, not really. I don't believe in them." His voice turned sober. "We're going to catch him. It's just a matter of time."

"Yeah, the sooner the better," Emily said under her breath.

Nick guided her inside where she poured them another cup of coffee and they returned to the sofa. Nick sipped his drink. "This stuff is delicious, soothing too."

"I'm glad you like it." Emily set down her empty cup.

He took his last sip then sat back and put his arm around her shoulder. Peace returned as they watched the embers burn away the night.

Just when Emily appeared content, without explanation she slid toward the other side of the sofa. "Look I don't want to bring up anything unnecessary while we're trying to rest, but I'm curious about a few things."

Nick sat up with military attention. "Sure, what would you like to know?"

"First, why aren't we looking for a dead body? I know I saw the trespasser carrying one."

How to convince her he was on her side? "I haven't asked Sheriff Rivers because I think I know the answer. If we catch this guy, we can probably get him to tell us where he buried the deceased."

Emily's breath hitched. "Really? You could do that?"

"Oh yeah, once we show him proof, and he confesses, it's all over."

"What proof do we have?"

"Your word, for one thing. We'll figure out his personality, learn what we can say to get him to tell all. Then we'll ask him questions to trip him up. Hopefully, he'll give us what we want."

"I see. So, if he thinks he's some sort of genius, you challenge him by saying he isn't smart enough to kill someone and hide the body."

Emily was as smart as she was beautiful. No wonder he melted inside when he let down his guard. He'd forced himself to keep a distance until he caught the criminal harassing her. He couldn't let his infatuation distract him until she was out of danger. Back to the dead body. After all she'd been through, she deserved answers regarding this case.

"You got it. While we realize we probably have a murderer in the woods, we're also concerned about the contents of the three-foot by one-foot steel box. Of course, we want to put this guy away before he commits another crime. At the same time, we don't want to spook the suspect into doing who knows what, maybe setting off a bomb that blows up the entire campground." Nick pulled Emily close. "I haven't mentioned our agenda because I don't want you to worry."

Emily laughed. "How could I not?" She rubbed her hands on her pants legs. "Do you really think there's a possibility of explosives?"

"Anything's possible. That's why we're taking every precaution. Once we locate the steel container, we'll call professionals to open it. Don't worry. I won't let you out of my sight." Nick pulled her next to him, let his lips meet hers. A light sensation rippled through him, filling the empty place in his soul. He never wanted to let go. His determination to protect Emily shot through him like lightning. He was more committed to finding the man in the cave than ever before. "I'm right next door. Don't worry, and get some rest." Nick gave Emily a good-night kiss on the cheek and left. So much for keeping his distance.

~

Even though Nick had gone, Emily still sensed his closeness, and she relaxed. Nick's attention pushed Donnie's rejection out of her life like a bad case of food poisoning. Had God sent Nick to lift her up so she wouldn't care about Donnie leaving or the gossip about the scene at the altar?

God brought good from bad. She'd heard it her entire life, but this was the first time she consciously experienced it happening to her. She shuddered to think what a disaster it would've been if she'd married Donnie and never met Nick. Well, God didn't let that happen. All too soon, she and Nick would go their separate ways. Whether or not she ever saw him again, nothing could ever separate him from her memories. Woven into her life, he was a part of it forever. What would tomorrow bring for her and Nick? For the investigation?

Chapter Nineteen

The next morning Nick whistled as he entered the office. All of a sudden, he stopped. It was the first time he'd whistled since Caroline died. The two of them had trilled the verses to their favorite songs. She had loved their duets. He could see her toss back her dark brown curls and laugh afterward. He cherished the memory, but that was all he had. All it was or ever could be. Caroline would be happier than anyone in Heaven to know he'd found someone to love. He finished the rest of the song and started on another one.

Even though he now agreed there was love at first sight, it had to grow to last. He bit his bottom lip. Soon Emily would return to Blue Mountain. He'd have to make time to go there. He intended to stay uppermost on her mind, even if it cost him nights of sleep when he returned to school and had to study until the wee hours of the morning. He yawned. Shoot. He was getting used to functioning on little to no sleep. He was okay with that because keeping Emily secure and catching the late-night digger were his main objectives.

Nick spooned grounds into the coffee maker and straightened his desk. By the time the aroma filled the room Sheriff Rivers showed up followed by Emily.

"Good morning." He waved as they entered.

Sheriff Rivers filled a mug with Nick's best attempt at morning Joe.

Emily declined. "I've already had some, thanks."

Nick couldn't keep from grinning when Emily refused. Unfortunately, she hadn't arrived soon enough to brew the good stuff.

After they sat down Nick hit the desk with his palm. "This creep's tried my patience. I'm more than ready to put an end to his roaming these hills. Of course, I realize the importance of locating the steel box Emily saw in the cave. Last night I thought of something my mother used to say when I lost something. I'd always tell her, 'It should be right here or over there.' She would say, 'Obviously, it's not where you think it is, or you would have it, so look where you don't think it is.'" Nick thumped a pencil on his desk. "Does that make sense?"

"Perfect sense." Sheriff Rivers held out his cup and grimaced after he took a swallow of his drink. Then he set the drink on Nick's desk. "With that in mind, Nick, you and I should cover an area of the forest we haven't searched."

Emily looked at Nick. "We've been through this before."

Nick directed his attention to Sheriff Rivers. "Right. And Emily. I still take full responsibility for her."

"I'm glad you're willing to do that. I agree she should go. She's still at greater risk alone than with us."

"Yeah." Emily couldn't keep disgust out of her tone. "Especially if I'm in my cabin and he breaks in again. Are both of you forgetting I came up with our best lead? I am a reporter…"

"Not now. We'll quibble later. Let's go." Nick motioned toward the door and they left for the woods.

~

As Emily walked amid the naked trees, she tried to put together the information surrounding this crime for the article she wanted to write for "Blue Mountain News." Unfortunately, the data flew around in her brain like confetti. She yearned to make sense of the little bits of material they'd discovered before it drove her nuts. She looked at Nick. "I'm convinced the man I saw in the cave killed someone, carried the body across my yard, and buried it in this forest. Too, as you said, I'm certain there's something dangerous in the steel container."

"Uh-huh."

"I believe he'd kill again to get the flash drive if he had to." Emily sucked in a big breath of air. "But why?"

"Now, that's something we'd all like to know. If we knew why, we'd probably know who was behind this and what they intended to do with the contents of the receptacle."

No wonder she couldn't figure it out. Investigating this illusive man was much more complicated than writing a piece about a crime after the police solved it and gave the facts to her. She usually interviewed the officer in charge of a case for updates to his investigation and her final news story. Sometimes she talked with the criminals after a trial.

Occasionally, she snooped on her own, but when she did, she had a specific lead or leads to follow. Once she interviewed a suspected crooked businessman. He let a name connected to money laundering slip. In his presence she didn't blink or let on she recognized the name. Later she contacted her connection in the police department, and they arrested the crook soon afterward. A sense of satisfaction rippled over her. This case was different though. This was like crawling around on the floor in the dark not knowing what might jump out at her next.

Sheriff Rivers halted and planted his hands on his hips. "Start paying close attention. We've reached a different region in the forest, an area I haven't visited in years, but there are two cascades to our right. As we get closer, we'll hear the rushing water." He let out a tiny gasp. "Rushing water, of course." He yanked the printed map out of his pocket. "The distance scale is greater than I thought when I first looked at this primitive drawing. These locations are going to be farther apart, but we're on the right track."

They gathered around the map and Sheriff Rivers rubbed his hand over the words rushing water. "Two waterfalls."

"Yeah." Nick pumped his fist. "Let's go."

The cascades roared down the granite hill, the sun shining on crystal-clear water splashes crashing against the rock into a fine mist. The sight took away Emily's breath. "God's power and glory dazzle here."

"Yes, they do, but we need to find out why someone noted this place on the flash drive," Sheriff Rivers said.

Emily walked around.

Nick caught up to her and took her arm. "Be careful. It's slick up here, especially where there's moss growing on the rock."

Nick's concern sent a sweet sensation through Emily. It failed to dampen her drive to root out another piece of this puzzle though. "I will." She climbed amid the smell of damp earth and a colder temperature. She would find something important if it was here.

She heard Nick and Sheriff Rivers talking but couldn't make out their words amid the cascades thundering against the hillside. When she stepped too close to the falls, the heavy spray hit her coat, but it was thick and water-resistant, so the dampness would not keep her from exploring. She stopped behind the falls, where water droplets fell on her knit cap.

After she'd rubbed the area rock by rock for twenty minutes, she found a loose stone and pulled it out. There was something behind it. Her hand trembled as she thrust it in the nook. Wait. Even though she wore gloves, they were dirty and might contaminate evidence. She jerked back her hand and pivoted to go tell Nick and Sheriff Rivers about her discovery.

Her foot slipped. She slid down the steep rock wall. Her pulse beat in her ears. She grabbed the end of a boulder, but barely hung on. Wiggling her leg, she touched a ledge with her toe. Would the ridge hold her? She planted both feet on it. Did she dare let go of the stone above her? She peered down then jerked her chin up. She couldn't look.

She couldn't stay stuck either. She took rasping breaths as she scanned the landscape. A small tree rooted in moss between the rocks grew a foot away. She leaned as far as she could to the right. Yes. She could reach it. Where would she go from there? She spotted a tiny overhang barely large enough to get the ball of her foot on. That was all she needed if she was careful. *Lord help me.*

Testing the tree's strength, she pulled it down. It

seemed strong enough. After she clasped one hand onto the sapling and held on with all her might, the other swung in mid-air. Her feet dangled below, shaking above her target.

Unable to hit the spot, she was like an airplane trying to land on a space barely big enough for a navy aircraft carrier. Each time her foot swung over the protruding granite she failed to make her mark and had to pull up her foot. Finally, she brushed the overhang with her toe. Yes. At last, she touched the small slab. *Balance. Balance.*

With every nerve in her body standing on end she prepared to jump, but hands wrapped around her waist. She fell backward into Nick's arms.

"For crying out loud, what are you doing up there?"

Trembling, Emily let out a loud, quivering laugh, partly because Nick's greeting startled her, but mostly from relief. "Umm." Barely able to speak she answered, "It just happened."

Nick hugged her. "Sit on this log and catch your breath." He pointed to a large fallen tree trunk.

Emily liked that idea. Her knees threatened to buckle underneath her.

"More things just happen to you than anyone I've ever seen. I can't help but think in most instances you help them along."

Nick wasn't usually rude. Trying to make light of her harrowing experience to keep from looking foolish, Emily jabbed his biceps. "That's not true. Besides, I found something important." She pulled back her shoulders. "And I didn't touch it, so you can test it for fingerprints."

Nick let out a loud "Ah. Hmm," then added, "I'm

glad you're alright. So, what did you find?"

In moments Sheriff Rivers joined them. "There you are. We've been looking all over for you. Don't let me regret allowing you to join us. My job is to take care of citizens not endanger them."

"I'll be more careful. I promise. Anyway, I got something."

Nick turned toward her. "Once again, what is it?"

Emily held her hands five inches apart, trying to illustrate the object as she talked. "It's a small, black carton, not nearly as big as the steel box I saw in the cave. I think it's plastic, but it's hard to tell. It's stuck in a hole behind a loose rock in the back of the waterfall on the right."

"You went back there sliding around by yourself?" Disbelief rang in Nick's voice.

Why wouldn't I? Nick was starting to irritate Emily, but she was determined not to get angry at him, even though he was making it more difficult by the minute. He did continue to take responsibility for her, or Sheriff Rivers couldn't have allowed her to come. She took a deep breath. "I've gone much worse places on my job." She pulled on her glove at the wrist. "Uh, well, maybe just as bad. Actually, I guess I haven't, but the point is…"

Nick's eyebrows formed a V over his nose. "You're going to have to stop acting reckless."

Emily retreated a few steps. "What? It didn't appear hazardous. It's not like I throw myself into dangerous situations. They just happen, like the man coming in my cabin. Having an intruder was much scarier than hiking around a waterfall."

"Cut it out. We need to examine whatever she

found," Sheriff Rivers said.

Nick assumed a military, at-attention stance. "Yes, sorry. Emily, why don't you tell us where to go?"

Emily pointed to their right. "It's over there."

"Okay." Sheriff Rivers scanned the immediate vicinity then wandered around the bottom of the falls for several minutes before he pointed to a trail. "This looks like a fairly clear path. Let's give it a try."

Emily put her hands over her face. "I don't know how I missed it. I just didn't see it."

Sheriff Rivers looked stone faced. She figured her oversight of the better route verified his reason for not wanting her along. Wait until he saw what she'd found though. She'd get a gold star when he saw it. With her pulse settling to a normal rate from getting down from the waterfall, Emily teased. "I'm all for it. I don't recommend the direction I chose." She chuckled.

Finally, Sheriff Rivers and Nick did too.

Within thirty-five minutes the three of them strode to the area behind the waterfall, where Emily showed them the loose rock.

Nick turned toward Sheriff Rivers. "Do you have a handkerchief?"

"Yep, and a bag too." Sheriff Rivers reached in a deep pocket in his coat, pulled out the items he needed, put on latex gloves, and retrieved the carton." He looked at Emily. "If you ever get tired of the crime beat at the newspaper and decide to go into law enforcement, I could use you up here."

Emily blinked. Sheriff Rivers trusted her after all.

"Noooo." Nick's voice echoed in the falls.

Sheriff Rivers laughed. "Well, she'd need a lot more training to work for us and something tells me she likes her job in Blue Mountain. I doubt you have anything to worry about."

He was right about her job, but she didn't know how much she'd like Blue Mountain without Nick. She glanced over at him. He was looking down at his boots. She could work alongside him in any investigation. He was smart, a great partner. More importantly, she trusted him to look out for her as she would him.

Sheriff Rivers stared at the small carton like a cat that just caught a rat. "I want to get this dusted and see what's in it. It's nearly five o'clock. Let's call it day."

They walked toward the Sky High office much faster on the return trip. When they reached Sheriff Rivers' car, he said. "See you later." Then he scooted in the driver's seat, waved, and left.

Nick put his arm around Emily's waist. "I'll take care of paperwork here then treat us to pizza. It's not often we have a chance to start an evening this early. What do you say?"

"We'll go to the little restaurant we can walk to, right?"

"Yes, but I hear we're getting gas soon."

"Great. What time do you want to go?"

"Seven o'clock?"

"See you then."

Nick went inside the manager's office and Emily walked to the cabin not sure which she looked forward to more—relaxing with Nick, or finding out what was in the black carton she found behind the waterfall. By the time she entered the quiet country kitchen, so empty without Nick's presence, she realized which she wanted more. At the same time, she sat on edge waiting for Sheriff Rivers' news. After all, she and Nick couldn't enjoy a normal dating relationship until they caught the trespasser and solved the mystery. She nearly fell off of a mountain locating that carton, so there was that too. Whew. Whatever dangers lay in her future, with Nick by her side she'd tackle them.

Chapter Twenty

Sitting in the small pizza parlor listening to Italian mood music while peering at Nick in the candlelight, Emily relaxed and let her spirts soar to the stars. This was more than the vacation she dreamed of when she came to Sky High Campground. This…this was surreal. Who would've thought romance could live in the midst of danger and chaos in a small tourist town in the North Carolina Mountains?

Maybe she had just been irresponsible in not filling up her gas tank when she arrived. Did God help her forget, so she'd get to know Nick, rather than simply driving out of town at the first sign of trouble? Guess she'd never find out for sure, but God had brought good from bad, and she was grateful.

Nick gazed at Emily with a caring glint in his eyes and the music danced in her heart.

"What had you planned to do while you are here. I'm sure your itinerary didn't include chasing a villain and missing night after night of sleep. None of our tourist brochures advertise falling into caves or slipping off of the side of a waterfall."

Emily held up her piece of pizza. "That's true, but…" She put down the food. "I think of this as high-level on the job training. I've done some unofficial investigating on my own for "Blue Mountain News." Most of the time I cover a crime after the fact." Emily tightened her mouth. "Actually, we don't have a lot of big-time criminals in Blue Mountain. Moments of terror notwithstanding, I'm learning a lot."

Nick propped his elbow on the table. "So, you think this is more than a run-of-the-mill local guy gone bad?"

"Yes. I've covered many stories about amateur law breakers. They're sloppy." Emily couldn't help but laugh. "One crook came to rob the Community Bank and wrote 'Give me the money' on a deposit slip with his address on it."

Nick laughed out loud. "Yeah, I've heard of those types of crimes."

"I think this man is different. He's smarter when it comes to criminal activity. If he was really smart, he'd lead a better life, but so far, on the dark side, he's stayed ahead of us."

Nick nodded. "He's slick. I know that. Our presence doesn't faze him in the least. He's moved around us as if we aren't even here." Nick fidgeted with his napkin. "His ability to outmaneuver us won't last forever. He'll make a mistake, possibly trip over his own arrogance. Take my word for it."

Emily leaned forward. "I hope he does it soon, but he's only one piece in a complicated puzzle." She sat back and took a sip of her drink.

Nick's lips turned down. "Yeah." He got a distant look in his eyes.

Emily regretted her words. She'd put a damper on an evening when she should continue to unwind and enjoy Nick's company. "But we're figuring it out. I predict his search for that flash drive, which we have, will cause his downfall."

"I agree he won't stop until he finds it, and we have it." Nick grinned. "Maybe we *are* a step in front of him."

They finished their dinner and left, the Italian songs drifting from the loudspeaker outdoors as they walked toward Emily's cabin. Nick pointed to a building all lit up in the distance. "That's the Hill Top Castle, known for fine dining. I want to take you there after the pumps are filled, and we won't have to go on fumes."

Emily gazed at the structure. "I'd love it. I'm happy most anywhere with the right person though. It's not where you go as much as who you go with." She gave Nick her most affectionate smile.

He hugged her. "For now, I'm your personal bodyguard, but after we have this guy in custody, we'll have more free time to ourselves."

They reached the cabin, and Nick said, "Call me if you need me."

"I'm not one bit worried. Go rest."

Nick gave her a good-night kiss and left.

She went inside and leaned against the door, the romantic music in the Italian pizza parlor replaying in her mind, filling her with joy and peace. Putting on her pajamas, sliding into bed, she recalled the nights she'd missed sleep because a ne'er-do-well kept her awake and invaded her privacy. The tranquility faded, and her entire body tensed, but tomorrow. She itched for tomorrow, to know what Sheriff Rivers would tell her and Nick.

The next morning when she awoke, the sun seeped under the bottom of the blinds on the bedroom window.

She sat up and stretched before she looked at the clock on the nightstand. She'd slept ten hours. Bounding out of bed, she hurriedly dressed and went to the kitchen to grab a protein bar when she noticed the drawer beside the sink was open. She didn't forget to close it, did she? No. She didn't leave things amiss when she went to bed. Well, as tired as she'd been she might have left it open.

No. It was closed. She was sure. She lived alone in Blue Mountain and checked everything out of habit. She did not leave that drawer open. She sucked in a fearful breath. *He broke in again and escaped without anyone seeing him, without even waking me.* She shivered as she grabbed her cabin key and rushed out the door.

She walked as fast as she could and charged up the steps to the manager's office. Entering panting, she blurted out, "Did you catch him?"

Nick stood beside his desk holding a piece of paper, which he put down, a bewildered look washing over his countenance. "No, why?"

"He was in my cabin. I thought maybe the officer patrolling had arrested him."

Nick plopped down in his chair. "In your cabin. Why didn't you call me?"

Emily fidgeted with the strap on her purse. "I didn't hear him. Either he crept around like a cat in bedroom slippers, or I was dead to the world last night. He left the drawer beside the sink in the kitchen open."

"If you didn't hear anything, maybe you forgot to close it." Nick folded his hands in front of him.

"I didn't." Emily gave him a harsh stare. "I didn't even go in the kitchen after I got back last night."

"Well think, maybe you opened it before we went for pizza."

Emily bristled. "Is this going to be like the deer he was carrying instead of a dead body."

Nick flipped his pencil down on the desk and let out a heavy sigh. "No. Did he take anything?"

"I don't know. I just thought maybe Sheriff Rivers' deputy picked him up. I practically ran all the way here to find out."

"I'm sorry that happened. We don't have him yet, but we will. Did you touch the drawer?"

"No, but it's simply pure luck I didn't. I was in a hurry to get here." Emily wanted Nick to do something so bad she couldn't stand still.

"I'll bring over the fingerprinting kit."

She allowed thoughts of success to flicker inside her, and her frazzled nerves settled. "Maybe it's worth having him break in if we finally find out who he is—and capture him."

Nick snatched up his office key and the kit, guided Emily out, and locked the door. When they walked into Emily's country kitchen, she pointed to the drawer. "That one."

She sat down at the table to watch Nick swish the brush around the drawer looking for

fingerprints.

He turned around. "He wiped it clean. There's not a single print."

Emily's shoulders slumped. "At least you believe me now. Obviously, I don't wash the drawers every day."

Nick pulled up a chair and joined her. "Right. Right. Right." He said the words in staccato rhythm then he pounded his fist on the table. "This man's a pro, or a pro's telling him what to do."

Nick's cell phone rang. He glimpsed it and leaned toward Emily. "It's Sheriff Rivers. Maybe he has good news." He answered, "Yes, sir."

Silence.

Nick's brow darkened with groves. "Okay, keep me informed, please."

Emily spread her hands apart. "What?"

"He ran the fingerprints off of the black carton you found at the waterfall. There's no match in the United States. He asked the F.B.I. for assistance, and they sent the prints to Interpol." Nick's voice trailed off. "What's going on?"

Emily shuffled her feet under the table. "I've never covered anything like this, but what would someone involved in international crime want in a campground next to a small town in North Carolina?"

Nick leaned back and peered into space. "I can't imagine, but now we know what we're up against."

Emily snapped her fingers. "Could we use the flash drive to draw him out?" She wove her hand into her hair and pulled. "Never mind. Since we don't know where he is, we have no way to lead him to the bait."

Nick placed his fingertips on his forehead. "Yes, we do. He's constantly hanging around the cabin. We'll leave a substitute flash drive where he can find it."

Emily wouldn't admit it to Nick, but the hair on her arms stood on end at the possibility of an international criminal lurking around her cabin again. She'd interviewed enough bad guys to know even the amateurs operated in a sub-culture she didn't understand. To think, this one hung out with a rat and carried around a dead body. At the same time, planting a USB was a great idea.

"We'll put false information on the flash drive and send him on a scavenger hunt. It will end when we turn him in to Sheriff Rivers." Nick hugged Emily. "You're a natural born detective."

Nick jumped up and hurried off while Emily sat gazing at the floor. Would this put an end to her ordeal and reveal the man as the murderer he was?

Chapter Twenty-One

Emily paced back and forth across the porch with her emotions clashing. When an image of the man carrying a corpse or petting the rat flashed in her mind, she started to shake. When she recalled getting trapped in the cave, she squeezed her eyelids shut, but when she thought of the intruder falling for the trick she and Nick planned, she stamped her feet. She couldn't wait.

Finally, Nick walked up the steps. "Afternoon. I purchased a flash drive and put a random file on it." He held it up.

Satisfied their plan would work, Emily smiled. "Perfect. Now we have to decide where to plant it. If it's too conspicuous he'll wonder if it's a trap. He won't pick it up. If it's hard to see, he won't notice it next time he drops by."

"Uninvited." Nick echoed Emily's cynicism before he stiffened. "Well, he's not visiting inside your cabin again. I'll see to that, but yes, we will find exactly the right place."

"He's come around so often I'm getting a read on his MO."

Nick scanned the area around the porch. "Tell me where to put the flash drive. We want it where he can easily see it, so he won't want to come inside."

"I'm definitely on board with that." Emily studied their surroundings. "Judging from the hide-out I fell into I'd say camouflage might work."

"Good idea."

"As much time as he's spent here, he probably knows the yard around this cabin better than I do. We should put it where he could've missed it, even if we have to create said environment."

Nick rubbed the flash drive between his thumb and forefinger. "Hmm."

Emily picked up a handful of pine bark chips the landscapers had placed around the shrubbery close to the cabin. "What about here? Maybe he'll think it's been in sight all along."

"If it had rained recently, that would work, but the past week's been unusually dry." He cast an intense gaze at the spot. "While we've had wind, it usually doesn't stir up pine bark this close to the house." He let out a throaty laugh. "But the animals do. I have it. It's a little gross, but we'll put on latex gloves and pick up droppings."

"Ewww. That's disgusting."

"I know. I know. I think he'll fall for it though."

"Ewww." Emily's knee-jerk reaction crept to the surface a second time. Yet, she owed it to Nick and herself to consider Nick's plan. She twisted a button on her coat. "You're right. Why not? Detectives go through garbage all the time."

"I'm going to the general store before it closes. Do you have a plastic bag?"

"Yes, I have plenty of garbage bags."

Nick hurried down the road.

Emily went inside, picked up a legal pad, and made notes. When her boss saw her story about this crime, however it turned out, he might give her a promotion, maybe covering all of the nearby towns. Who would've thought something like this would ever happen at Sky High Campground. There was a reason, and it was a big one. A national paper might even pick up this piece.

Well, she'd not let her imagination run wild. After all, it was technically still unsolved, so who knew how it would end? Absorbed in her writing, she didn't notice what time Nick left, but she barely finished her wrap-up paragraph before he returned.

She dreaded the collection, but followed Nick into the woods. He wore latex gloves, picked up droppings with a scooper, and shoved them in a bag. The entire ordeal amounted to very little exposure to the droppings, especially for her. She just watched.

When they returned to the cabin, Nick hosed the contaminated scooper and tossed it in the outside trashcan along with the gloves. Then he darted inside and washed his hands before he returned to the yard. After he scattered the pine bark with a rake and placed the flash drive in it, he and Emily stood back and eyed the creation.

"It's pretty realistic." Nick walked to the USB and pushed one end into the ground to make it appear someone had buried it and part of it had become dislodged. Emily held her nose while he poured out the contents of the bag, which turned out to be old with little to no odor. In no time it seemed, he finished.

"I'm going next door and take a shower." He left taking fast strides.

Emily figured watching the ordeal earned her a

bubble bath with essential oils, which she took before Nick returned.

After he arrived, she concocted dinner—French fries and turkey sandwiches.

"This reminds me of Saturday dinner in the house where I grew up. That was burger and Fries night."

"Ah, I'm glad it makes you feel at home."

"Watch out for any other devices hidden underneath the sink." Nick grinned as he sat down.

Emily gave him a thumbs up and joined him. Then Nick said a blessing.

"I can't wait for the suspect to come for that USB drive." Emily speared a French fry.

"Me either. I'd like to catch this guy tonight and end the harassment." Nick tapped his glass. "Ah, but on a lighter note, we have some delicious tea like your mom makes."

Emily smiled.

"By the way, the turkey sandwich hits the spot. Very good."

"I'm glad you like it."

Emily gulped down her entree and placed her hands on the table. "I don't want to miss this guy."

Nick ate his last French fry. "I hope we don't get indigestion from eating so fast, but I'm with you, let's clean this up and get in stake out position."

Within the next ten minutes the kitchen sparkled, and Nick and Emily sat on the sofa. Nick bounced his foot. "I'm ready to turn this guy over to Sheriff Rivers.

Nick's cell phone rang. He glanced at it. "Speaking of the sheriff, he's working late," he said before he answered.

"Yes sir."

Silence.

Nick cocked an eyebrow. "I understand. We do have something brewing here, we think. We purchased a flash drive with fake information on it and planted it around Emily's porch to lure this guy. If we can catch him, you're right. There's no telling where this could lead."

Nick hung up the phone and turned toward Emily. "It didn't take long for Interpol to give Sheriff Rivers the identity of the person whose fingerprints are on the small carton from the waterfall. They belong to a black-market arms dealer who goes by Joe Smithers." He scratched his chin. "I can't imagine his connection to Sky High Campground."

Emily tilted her head. "Me either. An arms dealer?" She let out a soft gasp. "What was in the container?"

"A million dollars-worth of uncut diamonds."

Emily shot straight up. "Payment for something. The flash drive tells the suspect where to find the diamonds. What I want to know—is the man who carried the corpse across my yard the same person who killed him?"

Nick's eyebrows edged toward his hairline. "I wish I knew. Chances are two criminals planned to sell the diamonds and split the money. Maybe one of them wanted it all. We have to take the investigation one step at a time and work with what we have."

"What about the arms dealer? If Sheriff Rivers contacts our government, can't they bring him here and interrogate him?"

"Nope. He's in Cuba. We don't have an extradition agreement with them. However, I'm sure we'll soon see the F.B.I. up here. I'd as soon bring in this guy myself if I get the chance."

A terrorist lived in a world so different from Emily's. And to think, someone who was one, or associated with one had been in her cabin. She cringed. "So, you're really thinking along the lines of terrorist?"

"That's a possibility, but either way, a local contact seems essential to any operation involving a person who isn't even in this country, but who is he? It's not Sheriff Rivers or Larry, and Danny Angeo's too busy feeding the town pizzas."

Emily rubbed her forefinger across her chin. "Maybe, it's one of the regular tourists."

"Um. Hmm. That's possible. Well, for now, we wait to see if anyone comes for the flash drive. Even if we can't extradite the arms dealer, the F.B.I. will find out more about him and how he's connected to these mountains."

Emily pushed up the sleeves on her sweater. "What's worth a million dollars in diamonds? Obviously, something in the steel box I saw in the cave, the murders, or both. What do you think?"

"My guess—the murder in Blue Mountain and the corpse you saw are casualties of the search for whatever's in that box." Nick checked his watch. "It's one o'clock. It doesn't look like our guy's coming tonight, or rather this morning."

"Of course not, the one time I want him to come, he can't be bothered."

"He'll turn up sooner or later." Nick gave Emily a flirty grin, pulled her to his shoulder, and hugged her. "I'm here. Try to rest."

~

Emily fell asleep on the sofa. When she awoke Nick

was gone and the door locked. She hopped up and went into the living area. He left a note on the coffee table saying he was only one call away. In the chaos he'd thrown so much office work on the back burner he probably had reports to finish for Larry. She respected his dedication.

Exhausted, she grabbed a blanket and pillow out of the hall closet and lay down on the couch, listening for the suspect to fall into their trap. Nothing but crickets. Her eyelids grew heavy. She dozed until she heard thuds on the porch.

She sat up and pressed her fists against her temples. Not again, but she would not cower or hide from him this time. Gathering her strength, she tip-toed to the kitchen and picked up an iron skillet.

Standing beside the entrance, she held up the pan with a trembling hand. Her muscles ached, but she would hit any intruder who entered her cabin. The hinges on the door wiggled. The pan shook in her hand. Heavy breathing drifted inside. Her legs grew as weak as gelatin. Suddenly the hinges stilled.

Letting out a sigh of relief she peeked out the crack in the drapes on the sliding glass door. The deputy sheriff's car drove by. She sank to the floor and the skillet plunked beside her. But how did he disappear so fast? Where was he? On weak legs she walked to the bathroom window. Did he lurk in the shadows the spotlights created on the side of the house? She clenched her fists. He wasn't there. Did she dare go on the porch?

She walked to the front of the cabin, opened the door enough to squeeze through, and took one stride outside. The moon still shone, but light started turning the Heavens toward day. She took a tentative step. Stopped. Turned around and went inside for her phone. A figure moving in the distance to her left ducked behind a large boulder then proceeded into the woods. She couldn't wait to tell Nick.

By the time she dressed, ate, straightened the cabin, and walked to the manager's office, Nick and Sheriff Rivers were deep into a conversation. She strode close to them to hear.

Sheriff Rivers said, "We haven't received any additional information from the F.B.I. since they told us the dead man in Blue Mountain was Surley Johnson, who grew up in Broken Arrow."

"Do they have more answers?" Emily tried to keep her voice from rising an octave to no avail.

Sheriff Rivers shrugged "Not enough. I informed them of everything we know. They're looking into this guy Joe and any associates in North Carolina. If I had to bet, I'd say Surley knew Joe, but that doesn't tell us anything about the man trespassing, or why he's carrying around a corpse."

Emily wanted to say, "I told you so," but the happiness swelling inside her because Sheriff Rivers finally believed she saw a dead body sufficed.

Nick slowly spread his hands apart. "And what's in the missing steel receptacle she saw in the cave?"

"For the life of me, I can't imagine what type of international crime could occur way up here." Sheriff Rivers scratched his chin. "It's odd, but I doubt whoever is roaming these hills is out to murder anyone unless they're in his way. He's focused on his mission, whatever it is. Apparently, he doesn't suspect we have the flash drive or the diamonds."

Nick pushed out his chest. "No, he clearly thinks the flash drive is in Emily's cabin."

Emily started to fidget. She had resisted giving them her information as long as she could. "I think I know the direction to take to find him if that helps."

Nick's mouth gaped. "How? What have you done now?"

Emily placed her hand on her hips. "*I* didn't do anything." She explained about someone on her porch. "I was going to call, but I decided to come to the office." She directed her gaze toward Sheriff Rivers. "The deputy you sent rode by, and the man ran away. It was barely dawn with limited visibility, but I watched him disappear into the shadows. I wanted to go after him…"

"Noooo." Rick and Sheriff Rivers replied in terrified tones at the same time.

Emily shrugged. "I thought better of it."

"Good" Sheriff Rivers' stern voice put an exclamation point on his words. "You need to leave it to us now." He pointed to himself then to Nick.

"Absolutely." Nick gave Emily a scolding look. "Sheriff Rivers and I will take it from here."

Emily held up her legal pad. "No, I'm covering this crime. After all, if it weren't for me, you two wouldn't know about it."

Sheriff Rivers glanced at Emily then Nick. "Covering it?"

"Yes, you forget. I work for the "Blue Mountain News." After you make an arrest, I'm going to write about it."

"We don't allow reporters to investigate crimes. We hold press conferences, but that's it."

"I need to show you which direction to take to look for him." Emily bristled. "Don't ask me to tell you where to go. There aren't any street signs in the woods."

Sheriff Rivers said, "Do you…?"

Nick nodded. "I still accept the responsibility for Emily."

"As we've said before, she's probably better off with us than she is alone."

"Especially, since the two of us planted a fake flash drive at her cabin."

"Whew." Sheriff Rivers swiped his forehead. "All right, I'll grab some items we might need from the office in Broken Arrow and meet the two of you at Emily's cabin at one o'clock."

Chapter Twenty-Two

Emily stood at the edge of the woods and motioned to the left. "He walked in that direction and disappeared behind that boulder." She pointed to ridges on the ground. "Even though they're faint, these footprints appear to point to the left. Do you still have the image of the soles of his tennis shoes?"

Sheriff Rivers patted the pockets on his pants and jacket. "Uh, yeah."

Emily shot him an expectant look.

"Yeah. Yeah. Here it is." He pulled the copy of the footprints from the inside of his jacket and opened it. "Sure 'nough, they're his."

Nick winked at Emily. "Good thing we brought her along."

"Uh, hmm, uh," Sheriff Rivers sputtered. "No argument."

They walked deeper into the barren, winter territory following the barely visible outline of the suspect's shoes, passing several large tree stumps, more pines, hardwoods, and rocks.

Something flew by Emily. She took a swat at it before she realized what it was. "A butterfly? I never would've thought I'd see one of those this time of year.”

Sheriff Rivers grinned. “It’s a mourning cloak. They live here in the winter and come out on warm days to entertain us and eat sap from the deciduous trees in the forest.”

“I see. At first, I thought it was an insect or a moth then I noticed the yellow trim around its brown wings.”

“Yes, some people say it draws its name from its color which supposedly represents mourning cloaks of those who’ve lost loved ones.”

Emily cast her gaze down. “That’s sad for them and the butterfly.”

Sheriff Rivers shrugged. “Doesn’t seem to bother the butterflies much.”

Nick laughed. “Okay, you two. There’s a cute squirrel perched on a log eating, but we’re not on a nature hike. We’re out here to catch a criminal.”

He was right, of course. At the same time, Emily originally had brought her boots because she wanted to frolic in the forest and take in the winter sights, not participate in an active investigation. Regardless, she would end up with a great piece for the paper, not that she had intended to work while away from the office either. The really good, fantastic surprise though, the one she’d least expected—meeting Nick, the highlight of this trip. She studied the marks on the ground. “I think they’re trailing off to the right?”

She and Nick walked around what remained of the prints for several moments then Sheriff Rivers held up and waved them over. “Try it this way.” He turned sideways and bent over. “You’ll get a better view.” He looked at it from the right and stood. When Emily did the same, he gave her a thumbs up.

They followed the disappearing splotches of the shoe soles for a mile up the mountain past foxholes, a cave, several huge stones, and a rocky creek running almost level with the ground. On the way, the only thing stirring—an occasional sparrow flitting from one barren tree limb to another. The imprints vanished completely as though a spaceship swooped the man to Mars. Emily placed her hands on her temples, her pulse beating in them in anger. She yearned to end this man's illegal activity, especially at her cabin.

The three of them halted and looked back and forth at each other.

Finally, Emily asked, "What do we do now?"

Sheriff Rivers wandered to the left then the right while Nick forged forward, both peering down as though they tried to sweep the forest floor with their gazes. Nick squatted and put his hands on his knees. "Over here."

She and Sheriff Rivers joined him. "I think he turned to the left, but these prints are almost gone."

Sheriff Rivers angled his body toward them and lifted a shoulder. "We can still work with this. Look closely at the underbrush for broken stems or a light underside on overturned leaves." He pointed to the hard-packed dirt and undergrowth beside him. "Notice the difference in the foliage when someone's walked on it."

Emily placed her forefinger on her cheek. Could he really find this escape artist by studying the dirt, bushes, and leaves?

"Even the rocks can tell us something." He picked one up, turned it over, and showed it to Nick and Emily. "This rock's exposed side is darker. That tells me it's been turned over, either by an animal or someone walking on it." He placed his foot beside an impression. "That's where it lay before it was disturbed."

Emily gave Sheriff Rivers several quick nods. He clearly knew what he was doing. "I've never thought about tracking anyone through the forest, but it's interesting."

"Yes ma'am. We have to know how to locate people in these hills. We have an advantage because there aren't as many folks roaming around these mountains this time of year. Considering we tracked this guy here, more than likely he's the one who disturbed the terrain, not an animal, or a homeless forest person."

"The technique will make a great addition to my story for the "Blue Mountain News." The community needs to know who's watching after them."

"Thank you, but that's not necessary. It's just part of the job. However, if you notice even the tiniest rearrangement of nature, let one of us know."

"I will. No one wants to put an end to this hoodlum's crimes more than I do."

Nick gave Emily a quick hug. Sheriff Rivers' eyes softened in the corners.

Getting close to wrapping up this mystery set Emily's mind on the story she would pen. She directed her gaze to Sheriff Rivers. "I may ask to interview you for a sidebar when I write my article about the capture of an international arms dealer."

"What? We suspect he has ties to an international criminal, but we don't know that for sure. Don't start writing until you have all of the facts."

"I won't. I don't present information for publication

until I know it's true, but that's what I think right now. I'd like permission to include how your expertise contributed to solving the case."

Sheriff Rivers threw up his palms. "I can't say 'no' to you. Maybe it's your smile. Maybe it's your personality. I don't know. Whatever, I guess it makes you a good reporter. One interview after it's all over."

Emily slung back her shoulders.

Nick laughed. "With everything you've been through, the least we can do is help you with a story."

Emily nodded in gratitude. "Thank you."

Sheriff Rivers sighed. "All right, let's keep it moving. Maybe we can wrap this up this afternoon."

"I'm on it," Emily said. Sheriff Rivers' words about tracking ran through her mind as she forged onward studying the environment around her.

"This guy's too smart to leave food wrappers or any other clutter, but if you come across any, it's a sure sign." Sheriff Rivers turned an admiring glance toward Emily. "But you'd have caught that even if I hadn't told you."

Acceptance at last. She grinned. "I probably would have."

As the three of them pressed onward, Emily stared at so many bushes and leaves and picked up so many rocks, visions of them danced in front of her as though she watched them in a video game. Nonetheless, she stayed on the task and spotted several groupings of underbrush that looked as though someone had banged into them.

When she squatted down and tried to find footprints, she couldn't because the dirt was too loose, but she spotted a rock with a dark side exposed. The only thing, what if she were wrong? Her inexperience could throw them off course. "Uh, Sheriff Rivers, I'm not sure about this, but maybe you should take a peek over here."

"You bet." He strode over followed by Nick. The two of them crouched down and examined the scene. "Hmm. I imagine a human passed by here, and my two cents says it's him." Sheriff Rivers stood. "I wish we could find a footprint."

Emily peered at the ground mumbling to herself in frustration. "If he hadn't scuffed up the earth, we'd have him, but he made a mistake somewhere. *We're going to find it.*"

"What are you talking about?" Nick's voice held a questioning tone.

She waved him off. "Nothing."

"It sounds like some type of analysis."

"No, it's more of a prediction." Emily visualized ridges on the bottoms of tennis shoes as she scrutinized the earth. Finally, she believed she saw some, but she'd looked so hard maybe she imagined them. She moved backward six inches and gave the spot the sideways look Sheriff Rivers showed them. "Yes!"

Nick and Sheriff Rivers darted to her. Sheriff Rivers pulled out the picture of the footprints. "It's him. Turn to the left." Excitement rang in his voice.

Obviously, this guy didn't intend for anyone to discover his new hideout. They'd made so many twists and turns she could have gone to the moon and back by now. She was glad Nick and Sheriff Rivers didn't leave her behind though. She stayed right with them as they continued deeper into the deserted forest, walking, observing the earth, rocks, and foliage until evening shadows crept across their path.

Emily wiggled her toes in her boots, trying to massage her tired feet. Even though she couldn't see as well this time of day and she'd never wanted to sit down as much as she did right now, she intended to force herself to go farther.

Nick walked to her. "Tired?"

Emily started to say "not too much" then decided to tell Nick the truth. "Very. I've examined so much ground for so long I have to strain to see anything."

"I know." Nick pulled her to his side. She leaned against his strong, firm shoulder. "Hey, Sheriff Rivers, should we should call it a night?"

"Yes. We've lost too much light." Disappointment resounded in his tone, his eyes glazed with a tired look.

Emily suspected she wasn't the only one struggling with exhaustion. Her body ached from squatting, standing, and walking for so long. She stretched, getting a moment's relief. As she wiggled her shoulders to relax, she let her gaze wander over the landscape. "Hey Nick, there's something to our right. In the shadow it looks like a boulder, but I think it's a mound of dirt. See it way back against the granite hill?"

Nick looked in the direction Emily indicated. "Yeah, how did we miss that?"

"It's a big forest." She motioned toward Sheriff Rivers. "I think he wants us to leave and start again tomorrow, but since we're here…"

"Sure." Nick called out, "Sheriff Rivers, come over here."

He hurried to Emily and Nick. "What ya' got?"

"We're not sure, but it looks like a mound of dirt." Nick turned toward Sheriff Rivers as Sheriff Rivers yanked a flashlight out of his jacket pocket and walked toward the spot."

Nick and Emily caught up to him. He studied a pile of soft earth while tapping his foot. "If this is a grave, why would he put it out here in plain sight?"

Nick scratched his head. "Maybe it was covered?"

"Huh? What are you thinking?"

Nick pointed to three large stones. "Maybe it means nothing, but those boulders are pretty close. I wonder if he put them over it when he first dug it."

"Yeah, maybe he hit so much rock, he decided to put it to use." Emily could hear the shovel banging against the granite in her yard in her brain.

Sheriff Rivers put on latex gloves, got on his hands and knees, and dug through the dirt until he hit a man's foot.

When Emily saw it, the bare trees spun, a black curtain falling across her vision as her legs gave way.

"Are you okay?" Nick caught her. "Sheriff Rivers, do you have water?"

"Yep. I come prepared. That's why I have big pockets in my jacket." Concern filled his voice. "Has she fainted?"

"I'm here," Emily managed to eke out.

Sheriff Rivers opened the bottle and gave it to Nick, who poured some on his handkerchief and placed it on the back of Emily's neck then rubbed her forehead with it.

When the world started to come into view, she held up her forefinger. "Hold that detective job. I'll stick to my articles."

Through the blurred landscape, she saw Sheriff Rivers cast a caring eye toward her. In moments he pulled out yellow tape.

Nick continued to place the makeshift cool pack on her neck and forehead and the world stabilized.

"I'm contacting the coroner and CSI. Even though there's no one out here now, we need to follow procedure. You know you're not to cross, go around, over, or under the tape."

"You don't need to worry about me. That foot sticking out of the ground is more than I need to see. I'm not about to encroach on any lines."

Nick patted Emily's shoulder and he and Sheriff Rivers shared an introspective smile.

Within no time the coroner and two CSI members arrived with flashlights.

The coroner, a tall man with graying hair and a runner's build, crouched around the body. "Rigor mortis has set in. This body's been dead a while, possibly a couple of weeks, and it's been moved."

I told them. Emily didn't want to rub in how many times she'd told them, but she couldn't resist cutting her eyes at Nick. "Uh-huh. As I suspected, the trespasser has moved the corpse all over these hills."

Nick's hand flew to his neck. "And uh, uh, you were right."

Come on. Are you going to acknowledge your early, unprofessional reaction?

"I should've believed you sooner."

Satisfaction swelled in Emily's chest. "That's okay." She grinned. "You've made up for it."

The coroner motioned toward the body. "See how the leg's sticking up. That wouldn't have happened after rigor mortis unless the body had been moved."

As soon as he pointed out the entire leg stuck in the

upward position, the scene started to swirl again for Emily. She must've looked pale to Nick because he took hold of her and pulled her away.

The coroner waved over the CSI members as Nick took hold of Sheriff Rivers' shoulder. "I'm sorry to interrupt. I assume you can take it from here." He tilted his head toward Emily. "I'm going to take her home."

"Yeah. Good idea. Be careful."

"Right. We will." Nick sounded as though he answered a commanding officer in the military before he switched on his flashlight then took Emily's hand to guide her away from the horror.

She took deep breaths of fresh air and grew alert again.

The coroner looked at Sheriff Rivers. "I'll let you know the cause of death as soon as possible."

Those were the last words Emily heard before they left the scene. Walking down the mountain, she sensed an evil presence hovering over them and her skin crawled. "My sixth sense tells me he's watching us and knows we found the body. If he has any reasoning ability, he'll wonder if we have the flash drive and diamonds. We are a target now."

"No more than we've ever been."

"He's probably more anxious now to find those diamonds and get away from here." Emily shivered. "I wish he would leave, but I don't want to say good-bye."

"Don't worry. We're going to have lots of help with the F.B.I involved." Nick stopped. "There's no telling who our mystery man is, or how much attention he'll get from people who have a lot more resources and expertise than we do. He's going to be too busy avoiding the F.B.I., to concern himself with you."

"He's so desperate to get the flash drive, he might come in the cabin again if he doesn't see the false USB we planted."

"I think he'll discover our little trap and fall for it, but either way, you're going to have plenty of protection. In addition to the F.B.I. roaming around, Sheriff Rivers will continue the night patrol." Nick rubbed his thumb over Emily's hand. "Then there's me. I won't let anything happen to you." He spoke in a soft tone.

A cozy sensation wrapped around Emily. "You're the best bodyguard a person could have."

Rustling nearby wafted into the night. Sticks broke and dead leaves crunched.

Nick stiffened.

"Did you hear something to our right," Emily whispered.

"Yeah. Stay here. I'll come right back."

Nick took off as though he'd been shot out of a cannon. Emily watched the glow from his flashlight fade into the forest as she paced in a circle wishing she'd followed him. He was a strong man trained in the military, but what if he was caught by surprise?

Cold air and blackness enveloped her. She reached in her pocket. No wait. She couldn't turn on the flashlight. If the suspect was the one making noise, she couldn't let him know where she was. She pulled back her hand. Twigs and branches broke. Animals scampered. What or who else lurked in the woods?

Where was Nick? He had some nerve telling her to wait here. In the distance she heard hollering. Her knees grew weak. Should she run to find Nick, or hide?

Chapter Twenty-Three

Nick tore through the forest. He'd like to get hold of this guy and tear him to shreds, but if he could catch him, he'd detain him and call Sheriff Rivers. No sign of him anywhere. Yet, he had to have a flashlight unless he had on night vision goggles. Nick held up and looked around. Never imagining he'd chase a killer through the North Carolina Mountains on his winter break, he left his night gear at school. He was at a disadvantage, but this wasn't the first time.

He'd taken out a sniper in Afghanistan when the sniper fired at him and other soldiers from a rooftop. He lost his night vision goggles on his way to the ramshackle house, which sat in complete darkness except for the flashes of gunfire popping around it. He gauged the distance he had left to go and took note of the shooter's position. It took longer than he'd been told it would, but he made it up a ladder to the roof of the house next door and took out the sniper with the first try. He gritted his teeth. He'd catch this guy.

He sat on a log covered in underbrush. Shined the flashlight behind him. No one. Good. He'd hear anyone approaching. He swung the light to his watch—eleven o'clock. He sensed the man's presence.

He and the man sat in the quiet, barren woods. Why didn't he show himself? Nick peered at his watch again—eleven-thirty. His hands burned to get hold of him. *Come on, you louse.* He would charge him on the spot. He wouldn't give him time to fall into a cave. His watch ticked to eleven forty-five. Had the man disappeared into thin air again?

Nothing stirred except the raccoons. He could sit here all night if he had to, but by now Emily's usual concern had probably turned to frantic worry. If he were in her place, he had to admit he'd want to see her now. Knowing her, if he didn't show up soon, she'd charge into the woods to look for him. He couldn't let that happen. He sighed and stood.

"Ha-ya! Ha-ya! Ha-ya!"

Nick rushed toward the sound. It was a small, battery-operated CD player. He picked it up. Threw it on the ground and stomped it. In his anger only after he decimated it, did he stop to consider it might have prints, but what good would a name do them anyway? Caves didn't have addresses. No, he was wrong and disgusted with himself for losing his temper and destroying evidence. He'd never done anything like that before, but he'd never cared as much about a person targeted by a criminal as he did Emily.

It took him only ten minutes to get back to her. She ran toward him as soon as the flashlight lit the edge of the path they'd been walking. Seeing her shaking with tears running down her cheeks, he grabbed his chest from the pain piercing it and turned away. He would never leave her alone all of a sudden like that again. He pulled her close and kissed her over and over. "I'm sorry. I was so furious at this guy for upsetting you, I let my emotions cloud my judgment. It won't happen again."

"Okay." Her voice weak, she sounded devastated.

He wanted to crawl in a wormhole, which only doubled his anger at the vile man tormenting her. He hoped Sheriff Rivers would find a way to bring the man in because if it were up to him, it wouldn't be a pretty sight.

"I promise I'll take better care of you."

Emily leaned against him.

Thank you, God, for keeping her safe.

"We realized he was running away from not toward us. I heard hollering in the distance though. What happened?" Emily's voice sounded a little stronger this time.

Nick took a deep breath and exhaled. "Yeah. He gave me the slip again. The ha-ya came from a recording. This is no amateur, but don't worry, we're on to him. The more he taunts us the closer we get. It isn't far to the cabin from here. When we get there, I'll fix us soup, or my coffee, or anything you want."

"Your coffee. First you leave me in the woods. Now you're going to fix me your coffee?" She snickered.

She was alright. "Okay, you can get our drinks. I'll whip up something for us to eat." He hoped to get soup for Emily for a long time.

~

Emily started their brew and placed a can of creamy potato soup on the counter before she collapsed on the sofa. Exhausted, she stayed put and waited to see if Nick's word about preparing something to eat was good.

Alone in that forest, missing him, worrying about

him, she realized how much she cared for him, but she would never give another man her heart until she knew he meant what he said. Poor Nick had Donnie to thank for that. It wasn't Nick's fault, but that's the way it was.

Tonight, she could've easily turned on her flashlight and followed the path to Sky High. With every sensibility she possessed, she grew anxious and stayed until she saw Nick because she wanted to. She'd nearly crumbled when she heard yelling because she feared for his life. That's when she started to shake and couldn't hold in the tears. She was no damsel in distress, even though she'd never been so tired in her entire life. That's why she needed Nick to keep his word about fixing the soup.

He meandered around washing his hands in the sink then coming over to put his arm around her shoulder with her focusing on him then the soup can all the while.

"Don't worry, please. We're so close to getting this guy."

Emily could hardly pay attention to what he was saying for looking at the soup can. "Uh, probably. When you chased him through the woods tonight, he knew you were closing in on him, or he wouldn't have put out the recording and snuck off."

Nick bit his bottom lip. "You're right."

What about the soup? The coffee maker gurgled. Emily looked in that direction then directed her gaze at Nick. "Well, our drinks are almost ready."

"Right, and I was going to make soup."

Emily took a sigh of relief.

"Is this it?" He picked up the can. "Ah, yes, something to warm us. Why don't you rest while I get this. Then you pour our drinks, grab some bowls for us, and we'll eat." Nick sounded happy when he said we'll eat. He was probably starving after all they'd done.

"Thank you." He had no idea how close he came to losing her trust.

The soup cooked in minutes then Nick said a blessing, and they ate. When Emily propped her elbow on the kitchen table and put her chin on her fist, it slipped off. "I have to go to bed soon. I'm wiped out," she said as she straightened up.

"Me too. I'm beat. The patrol car just passed. I'm sure Sheriff Rivers let everyone know about the latest body. Our murderer's bound to realize it would be a bad idea to show up right now." Nick stood and put his hands on his hips. "Oh, don't get me wrong. He won't stop until he has that flash drive, but not tonight. This cabin and yard are too hot for him right now."

Nick patted Emily's shoulder. "But here I am going on and on when you need to get to bed." His gaze lingered over her. "He made this personal for me when he invaded your space." He narrowed his eyes. "But soon we won't have to contend with him."

He put his arms around Emily, trailed his finger down her cheek, and kissed her with passion. "He won't get within ten feet of you," he whispered before he let her go. Joy she'd never known before swelled in her chest.

After she walked him to the door, she straightened the kitchen, happiness bubbling inside her as she eyed the soup can before dropping it in the trash. Now, to get a good night's sleep.

~

The next morning Emily threw back the covers on

her bed and stretched, her gaze falling on the clock on the nightstand. She had slept ten hours and awakened refreshed. She breathed deep. Bounding up, she could hardly wait to find out what Nick had heard from Sheriff Rivers.

After she tugged on a pair of jeans and a T-shirt she rushed into the kitchen, where she got the midnight coffee out of the fridge and microwaved a cup to go with a bagel, gulping it down.

When she arrived at the manager's office, Sheriff Rivers had his hand on the corner of Nick's desk, peering at Nick with intensity. "According to the F.B.I., Surley recently made a trip to Africa and contacted Joe afterward. The F.B.I. has no idea why. Since Joe's an arms dealer, the officials are trying to place Surley in Africa selling guns and weapons. So far that's led nowhere. I gave them Emily's statement saying the steel box isn't big enough to hold guns. They want a description of it." He looked up. "Ah, there she is now. Emily, could you give us more details about the steel object you saw in the suspect's cave?"

"I'll try."

Sheriff Rivers sat down in a chair in front of Nick's desk. Emily sank into one beside him and Nick joined them.

This was important. If she never got anything right again, she could not mess this up. She slammed her eyelids shut to visualize the scene in the cave. She opened them and said, "I'm doing this from memory. I was frightened, but I'll do the best I can." She cleared her throat. "The container was definitely some type of metal, as I said, steel, I think."

Sheriff Rivers made a note and looked up. "What

about the size?"

She spread her hands apart. "I estimated it at three feet wide, three feet deep, and a foot long." She lifted her eyebrows. "It could've held small handguns, I suppose. There's no way anyone could've put rifles in it."

Sheriff Rivers pulled at his ear. "Um, hmm. So you believe the receptacle was steel."

"Yes, that's what it looked like to me, but of course I'm not sure about that." She wished she understood more about different types of metal, but she was pretty certain it wasn't aluminum. "I suppose it could be lead."

"There could be a bomb inside." Sheriff Rivers sat back and rubbed his hands on his knees. "People also enclose radioactive material in steel or lead."

Emily's insides coiled as tight as an overwound watch. "As in a nuclear bomb?"

"It's possible." Sheriff Rivers tried to sound matter of fact, but Emily heard fear in his tone. "We'll let the F.B.I. decide if they need an EOD tech to disarm a bomb, or a hazmat team to dispose of something like uranium. We can continue to look for the container, but if we find it, we'll contact them immediately. We should not touch it."

Emily's muscles loosened in relief knowing someone else would search for the box. Bombing and black-market uranium were way out of her snooping range, but she did want the details after all was said and done—the sooner the better.

"I'm leaving for Broken Arrow to speak with the coroner. I want to take another look at the cave where Emily hid. I'll stop by if you'd like to go, or I'll call if I can't make it."

"Thank you. I'd appreciate that," Nick said.

"Sure thing. In the meantime, watch out for this guy." Sheriff Rivers stood. "All right then, we'll talk later."

After Sheriff Rivers left, Nick crossed his arms over his chest. "So, we have Surley Johnson from Broken Arrow to thank for this. What better place to store radioactive material than in a cave?" He walked from behind his desk and planted his feet wide. "Now we need to find his new hideout and get him to tell us who ordered the suspected uranium, or bomb. I thought we were close to solving this. We've only begun. Begin we will though—with great resolve."

Even though Emily's stomach fluttered as if a thousand mourning cloaks invaded it, she wanted to find the box, not touch it, not even get close to it, but find it. "Let's look around the woods for another cave."

Nick ran the tips of his fingers over his mousepad. "I can't let you endanger yourself anymore."

"I'll admit I've never dug up, no pun intended, a story like this. At the same time, you're underestimating me because I didn't deal well with a dead body. I can still help."

Emily rattled on. "It was the foot. When I saw it sticking out of that pile of dirt, it looked unreal." She scrunched up her shoulders. "It was like…Well, like I thought he moved after he was already dead, like he was trying to kick out of the earth or something. Whatever, I'm over it now."

"All right. Meet me here around three o'clock."

Chapter Twenty-Four

Emily arrived at the manager's office promptly at three o'clock. Visions of finding another clue to wrap up the investigation flashed in her mind.

Nick rose from the chair behind his desk, grabbed his coat, and put his arms in the sleeves on the way out. "I'm ready to put a stop to this."

Emily kicked a rock out of her path. "Have you heard anything new from Sheriff Rivers?"

"No. He's tied up talking to so many law enforcement officials he can't make it here today. I suppose we should wait for him, but I can't. I have to do my part to assure no one will set off a nuclear bomb."

When they reached the edge of the woods, Emily scanned the vast forest. "Where do you want to start? We know one place the container isn't." She held up her forefinger. "Unless, he returned the stuff to the cave thinking we wouldn't look there again."

"Hmm. It won't hurt to take another peek."

They trekked into the woods until they reached the abandoned hideout, the underbrush once covering it scattered all over the ground. "There's probably nothing here, but why don't you wait while I make sure?"

"Okay." Emily had spent more than enough time in that hole.

Nick grasped the huge tree root and lowered himself. Without the camouflage Emily could see part of the way into the cave. It appeared deserted. She watched Nick take cautious steps toward the area where the steel object had been until he disappeared from her view. Then she sat on a large tree stump and watched one squirrel chase another ruffling the brown leaves as they scampered through them. By the end of March these woods would burst in color, not only the green leaves, but the mountain laurel, daffodils, and pansies. Maybe she would come again for a long weekend, possibly to enjoy the Apple Blossom Festivities.

Nick emerged brushing off his pants. "As we thought. Let's hike up the mountain to the waterfalls where you found the diamonds. While we're there we might as well take another look at the grave site."

"Okay." Emily walked beside Nick. "As meticulous and cautious as this Houdini artist is, I can't imagine why he put the dead man's body in a mound of dirt that looks like a grave."

"Yeah, I've asked myself if he wanted us to find the body to distract us from the steel box. His attempt to bury the guy was sloppy. Animals probably dug around the boulders, pushed them over, and unearthed the corpse. What I want to know—who was the deceased? I thought I'd hear from Sheriff Rivers earlier. He was talking to the F.B.I. this morning."

"Hopefully the authorities will give him the man's ID soon. I'm sure he'll tell you as soon as he knows." Emily gazed around. "I wouldn't mind a hike to the waterfalls even if we weren't trying to unravel a mystery.”

"I'm sorry you've missed so much of your vacation."

Emily twirled her bracelet. "The trip's had rewards." Meeting someone as kind as Nick, having him completely wipe away every tear Donnie caused was the big prize for her, more than she expected when she left Blue Mountain. "If we can get this guy, I'll leave happy."

By the time they were halfway up the steep hill, with no leaves on the trees to muffle sound, Emily heard the water crashing against the rocks. God's power roared into the quiet and she forgot about the evil lurking in the hills.

When they reached the top, as she started to search for the missing steel item she'd seen in the cave, she focused with intensity on locating the box. She and Nick studied the terrain near the pool where the water fell for a good hour.

Nick let out a heavy sigh. "I don't think it's here."

"I wore my waterproof raincoat. I'll slip behind the falls for a closer look."

"I see the reporter coming out in you."

Emily grinned. "I'll only take a few minutes."

A short hike on the route Sheriff Rivers had shown them put her behind the cascades, where she sensed God's strength and omnipotence once more. How had this depraved person killing people missed knowing God? Rubbing her hand along the rear wall, she looked for a loose piece of granite or a wobbly boulder. Clearly, the criminal *didn't* know God, or he would've lived a different life. What was worse, on this earth thus far he had killed, stolen, and done any number of reprehensible things, which he appeared to have gotten away with. Yet, in the end, he could only lose. She swiped a rock firmly in place when she thought she heard Nick calling her.

She walked back to him. "I didn't quite finish, but so far there's nothing new here."

Nick patted her shoulder. "That's all right. Rivers called. After he gave the F.B.I. your description, they informed him they would send an EOD specialist and a hazmat team. We're done."

"Thank goodness, but what if the box is a false alarm?"

Nick cocked an eyebrow. "I'm ninety-nine-point-nine percent certain it isn't. Even if it is, it's too risky for them to take a chance it's nothing. They can't ignore your report, or the imprints Sheriff Rivers asked CSI to make."

"Right. He did do that. The entire discovery isn't on me." If she had led the F.B.I. to a dead end, at least she shared the responsibility with Sheriff Rivers and CSI. "So, what should we do for the remainder of the day?"

"Sheriff Rivers wants me to meet him at the manager's office."

Emily pointed to the path leading to the bottom of the hill. "Then let's go. I'll come too."

"All right."

By the time they reached the office and Nick unlocked the door, Sheriff Rivers arrived.

"Hi, I'll make coffee if you like," Emily said.

Sheriff Rivers gave Emily a quick nod. "I would. That sounds wonderful."

Nick scooted behind his desk and pointed to a chair. "Have a seat. We're all ears."

"It's been a busy day to say the least. My contact at the F.B.I. tells me they aim to search day and night until they find the steel box."

Emily served the coffee. "I hope it's not a false alarm. I don't think it is though. As for me, I'd rather not glow in the dark or get blown up." She set down her cup and joined Nick and Sheriff Rivers.

"That's not going to happen." Nick answered with a voice that held the strength of iron. "So," he peered at Sheriff Rivers. "Have they come up with a name for the murdered guy we found? Surely someone's looking for him."

Sheriff Rivers took a sip of his drink and contentment washed over his countenance. He winked at Emily. "Ah, thank you."

"You're welcome."

"To answer your question, yes." Sheriff Rivers' brows perched low. "It was Josh Roggue alias Tough Guy Roggue." He shook his head. "I can't imagine who could've killed him." He took another sip of his coffee. "Umm. That's good." He swallowed. "If Surley and Roggue had both wanted all of the money for whatever deal they had going with Joe, I'd say I had a motive and figure one of them murdered the other guy. With both of them dead, I have to admit, I don't have a suspect in mind." Sheriff Rivers set down his cup.

That was puzzling. What did Nick think? Emily turned toward him. He looked stone-faced.

Nick took in a deep breath and blew it out. "I see what you mean."

Sheriff Rivers steepled his fingers. "The only explanation is one of them, either Surley or Tough Guy, confided in another person who's looking for the flash drive and diamonds. The precious stones are probably payment for something."

"Right. We can't let down our guard. We need to collect every bit of evidence as soon as possible."

Sheriff Rivers slammed his fist on Nick's desk. "Absolutely. Believe me, I won't let him escape. I want to arrest the scoundrel right here." He scooted his chair backward. "Of course, one would think he'd leave as soon as he saw the F.B.I. He's after that flash drive though. He's slick, or he's getting directions from Joe. Either way in my opinion, he's arrogant, thinking he's outsmarted us every step of the way. I intend to get him before he escapes these hills." Sheriff Rivers stood. "That's it for today. See you later."

"Stay in touch," Nick said.

"Yes, you too, please." Sheriff Rivers left.

Nick locked up the office. He and Emily strolled to her cabin, where she stopped on the porch. "I wonder if our fake flash drive is still here." She walked to the area where they'd partially hidden the item in the pine bark. "It is. I can't believe he hasn't found it."

Nick leaned in. "He'll come for it. With everything going on I'd say he'll do it soon."

Emily bent over and studied their set up.

Nick knelt down. "Looks undisturbed to me."

Emily nodded. "Yeah, it's still intact."

Nick stood and brushed off his hands. "I agree with Sheriff Rivers. Our guy believes we can't catch him. It's apparent he knows a lot about these hills. At the same time, the F.B.I. is an added stressor, and now, the hazmat team. The heat's on. He'll have to decide whether to find the flash drive *and* the diamonds or get the flash drive and try to disappear. I believe he'll wait and look for the diamonds when things cool off. He won't leave them behind forever. He murdered for them."

Emily nodded. "Okay, so what do we do?"

"We wait. When it gets dark, we'll turn out all of the lights and sit up all night if we have to."

"Sometimes I wonder if he watches us."

Nick remained silent, his gaze clouded and distant. Finally, he said, "Maybe we should take that into consideration. Let's leave and stay in the manager's office until it gets dark. Then, we'll sneak into your cabin."

"I'm game."

"I'll deal with him and any other unwanted guests." Nick made a fist with his right hand and pounded it into his left "I won't lose him this time."

Chapter Twenty-Five

At five o'clock Emily washed out the coffee pot and cleaned up the refreshment area in the manager's office. Nick straightened his desk, got up, and helped Emily with her coat. After he slipped on his, he picked up his Glock 22. Emily gasped. When she'd sleuthed a bit on her own for the "Blue Mountain News," she'd never carried a gun. She didn't even own one.

Nick pulled her into a side hug. "Since we're going after a guy we suspect of murder, having a weapon gives me a sense of security."

Nick's assertive tone resounded in Emily's mind. As a military intelligence man and a security guard, he knew how to handle the gun. "You're right, of course. We have to protect ourselves. I'm glad you're bringing it because I believe he will show up, especially if he doesn't know we're there."

Nick studied her for a moment then glanced at the gun. "Don't worry. I'll only use it if it's necessary."

"Okay." It surprised her how much she trusted Nick, even with a firearm. After what happened between her and Donnie, she never thought she'd trust any man. Donnie. She puckered her mouth. He didn't matter anymore.

Nick locked the door from the inside and turned around. "We'll exit out the rear of the building. I'm going to leave a few lights on to make it appear I'm working late."

"He might buy it."

"Any better ideas?"

"Nope. Let's try it."

"We'll go to the cabin a back way he might not know."

"Okay."

They slipped out and strode in the shadows of the moon and stars, Nick cutting his flashlight to dim, pointing it down. "Walk slow, try to keep quiet, and stay near me."

Emily stepped right next to him. He put his arm around her waist, and they crept along. Knowing a murderer watching them might lurk nearby in the woods sent a chill up Emily's spine. The leaves to her right rustled. She jumped and grasped Nick's arm.

He stopped short and pulled her closer to him.

She looked up. A pair of big orbs stared at them. She gasped and stumbled. "Over…over." She pointed. "Look over there."

Nick turned to a forty-five-degree angle. "Hmm. The large, scary eyes belong to a mountain lion. Their pupils open extra wide at night. He sees us, but apparently, he isn't hungry."

Emily gazed at the huge animal. "I'm thankful for whatever he just ate. I'm not sure which is more dangerous the mountain lion or the murderer."

Nick stiffened. "I see your point. They're both killers, but you're forgetting, I have a gun. Believe me, if I need to, I can shoot that mountain lion."

Emily breathed a sigh of relief he'd brought the weapon. "Thank you. Technically, we're the ones interrupting *his* evening on *his* turf. Let's leave him in peace as long as he doesn't bother us. If we can make it to the cabin, we're set for the night."

Nick nudged her. "We're good, I promise. Remember when the man we want to trap sees me, he disappears."

Emily clamped her jaws to suppress her laugh, but a snort broke through and eked out.

"Quiet down."

Another one escaped.

"Stop."

"Okay." Emily wasn't sure if she giggled at Nick's attempt to lighten the air or to cover her fear, but she quit.

Finally, they reached the rear of the cabin, where Nick stood for a moment surveying the structure. "Is there an unlocked window anywhere?"

"I hope not."

"Think. We need to go inside without using the front door in case he's watching the house."

"Oh, you're right." Emily scratched her head. "Since he's already come inside uninvited, I've kept all of the windows locked, but the lock on the bathroom window has come loose. Maybe we can break in there. I should've reported it and asked for a new one, but with everything going on…"

Nick put his fingers over her lips. "Shh. That's great. I'll try to wiggle it free."

They moved slowly with the moonglow and stars lighting their way to the bathroom window, where Nick turned on the flashlight. He stood on a small shed for storing logs and fiddled with the lock. In what seemed like an hour, but was probably only ten minutes, he hopped down and gazed at Emily. "Okay, go for it."

Emily bristled. "Me?"

Nick swung his arm over his body. "Yes. I can't possibly get through that small space."

"Oh right, I see your point, but I…" Emily stuttered. "I, uh, I'm not accustomed to entering homes through windows."

Nick looked up. "It's a little high, but I'll climb on the woodshed with you. I left the window open so you could get in easily."

"We can't see out here."

"Not ideal circumstances, I agree. How about this? I'll point the flashlight right at the window. Then I'll I pick you up and push you through."

Emily started to see herself as a piece of celery punched into a juicer. At least he would make sure he forced her into the open window and not the side of the house, she hoped.

"We can't take the chance he's watching the front of the house. Trust me, this is the best thing to do. I'll make sure you enter in one piece."

Though she never doubted his intentions for a second, she, not he, had to deal with the consequences if his efforts failed. "Okay, how do I go hands first over a toilet into a house with no lights?"

"Don't. Do it feet first a little at a time. Locate the back of the tank with the toes of your shoes then very carefully lower your body until you can put one foot on each side of the seat. You can balance by holding the window jamb."

If Emily's vocal cords hadn't been frozen in fear,

she would've laughed at the ridiculous suggestion. "I know he's really slick. Of course, we have to figure out what he'll do next and stay one step ahead of him. You and I have to get in the cabin and wait without him knowing anyone's there." She almost talked herself into it. "This wasn't what I had in mind, but I'll do it." There.

"How about a nightlight. Do you have one in the bedroom or bathroom?"

"Uh, yes." A spattering of optimism swept over Emily. "I'll stay near the window until my vision adjusts." *Hopefully, I can see well enough to pull this off.*

"Good."

Nick helped Emily onto the woodshed and positioned her right in front of the bathroom window. "Are you ready?"

A strong wind whipped around her. Ready? No. She sat down, the breeze chilling her will to complete the task. If she didn't see it through, they'd probably not nab the trespasser. She took a deep breath. "Yes. Go ahead."

Nick lifted her toward the opened window, balancing her in the air until her feet were inside. She grabbed both sides of the window frame. Her body stiffened as though it had no intentions of going through. She loosened her muscles, bent her knees, and let her feet dangle above the toilet. She had to move farther down on each side of the window for her toes to touch the seat. Her body shook.

"Move one hand down then the other."

Nick didn't understand. She attached her hands to the jamb as though she'd put them in wet cement. She lowered her gaze. He was right. She couldn't stay halfway in the window. She had to go in or out. In moments she let go with her right hand and clasped the side of the window a bit lower. She was lopsided, but her right foot touched the seat. *Good job, Emily.*

She repeated the process then used the seat like a stepping stone and sprang off with her feet flat on the floor, her arms waving. She'd had many out-of-the-ordinary, snoopy moments covering her crime beat. She even spent a night crouched by a window hidden in the bushes outside of a home watching a burglary take place. After she informed the police, she stayed for the arrest, which made her article a lot more interesting than reporting it after the fact, but this…this was like nothing she'd ever covered. *Pulitzer Prize here I come.*

She walked to the front door and let Nick inside.

He high-fived her. "Great job. Now, we wait."

"In the dark?"

"Yes. If we talk, we have to whisper."

"I see. This is like a stake-out, except it's a stake-in."

Nick muffled a snort. "Save it for your article. Whatever we call it, it's worth the effort. He'll show."

"I'm going to sit on the sofa and peep through the crack in the curtains, even though he's so noisy, I'm sure we'll know he's here without me spotting him." Emily sat down and stared at the large, sliding glass door.

Nick joined her. "We have to stay quiet if we want him to believe we're at the office."

"I know." After peering at the open space between the drapery panels for thirty minutes, Emily nodded off. She jerked up though. She would not fall asleep.

Despite the drama, this vacation had turned her life around and put her on a happy path. She had Nick to thank for that. Then there was the story for "Blue Mountain News." She yearned to catch this guy and get on with her vacation and her new life. As her chin headed for her chest again, she heard a loud thud on the porch. She jumped up as though someone put a firecracker under her. "Was that…?"

Nick shot off of the sofa. Yet he tip-toed to the door then glanced over his shoulder and mouthed, "It's him. Stay put."

Chapter Twenty-Six

A thump from outside resounded in the living area of the cabin. Emily dashed to the sliding glass door, opened the slit between the curtain panels an inch, and peeked out. A scream caught in her throat. The man with the long hair stomped underneath the glow of the moonlight and up the steps to the porch. He paced in and out of the dim light next to the door. He rubbed the planks on the house as though he thought one of them might be loose.

Chewing on a knuckle, Emily scanned the porch for Nick. Did he find a pitch-dark corner and hide in it? Why didn't he go ahead and jump this guy? Was the thump…? Noooo. If she didn't see Nick in a few seconds, she was going outside and tear that monster to bits.

She leaned closer into the window. Nick was nowhere in sight while the guy walked around at will. Her breath grew so ragged she wondered if the suspect could hear her. She had to do something. She tip-toed into the kitchen and grabbed the cast iron frying pan. As she returned, a scuffle like a mountain lion charging an elk wafted from the porch. She peeked out. The man tumbled with Nick, the man's hair flying back and forth.

She flung open the front door. The man flashed her a poison-tipped stare, his eyes wild, his hair swishing. She raised the pan. The man yanked Nick over. She lowered the pan. "Get in the cabin," Nick grunted.

"Not on your life." She raised the skillet again.

The man twisted, made a move for a gun stuck underneath his belt. Emily nearly dropped her weapon. Nick slammed the man onto the porch, got on the guy's back and reached for the Glock 22. The man rolled over and pinned Nick on the planks. Emily held up the pan ready to strike. Why didn't Nick throw him off? The man held Nick down and went for his gun, his fingertips on it. Nick pushed up and tossed the man to the porch floor. The man rolled over and balled his hand into a fist. Aimed it at Nick's jaw.

"No you don't." Emily let him have it.

The man's eyes dimmed.

She drew back to hit him again.

"That's enough." Nick removed the man's gun then turned him over and handcuffed him. "I got him." He yanked up the killer, shoved him into a rocking chair and stared at him. "Don't you dare move. Emily, watch him while I call Sheriff Rivers."

Keeping a firm grip on the iron skillet at her side, Emily glared at the trespasser. Then she cast her gaze at the cookware. She didn't need a gun.

She focused on the man's twisted half smile. What turned him into a criminal? If she had run into him in the general store, she might think he needed to shave and put on clean clothes. Otherwise, he looked just like any other shopper—dark brown hair, a straight nose, and a small mouth. The more important question was—

what had gone wrong with his heart? His mind?

"You're staring at me. Ain't ye' ever seen a mountain man before?"

Emily wanted to know more about him for her story, but she couldn't force a single question from her scratchy throat. She'd never gotten this close to someone who murdered two people. Nearly gagging, she made a choking noise. She swallowed. "I've seen lots of mountain people. I'm one myself, but I haven't known many killers. What's it like?"

Wrinkles assembled on the man's brow. "Just like any other job. You do what you gotta' do to survive."

A mountain boulder couldn't have hit Emily any harder than the man's words. "That's not like any other job. It's a sin."

The man laughed. "A sin, you say." He leaned forward.

Emily flinched and aimed the frying pan.

The man sat back. "What about you? I bet you sin too?"

"Of course, I do, but I don't believe in harming any of God's creatures, especially people."

"Well then, you're a good person to take care of my rat."

Emily gasped. "I don't like rats. I'm afraid of them."

The man's chin quivered. "Please, could you just feed him. All the stuff I've done ain't his fault. He's a sweet, tame little rodent. He won't hurt you."

This man loved that rat. A voice in the back of Emily's mind told her to show compassion. Had she heard right? No. She wasn't thinking clearly after the events of the evening. Her conscience played a tug of war with her heart and good sense. Good sense was losing. "I'll tell you what."

He sat up straight. "Yes."

"I'll trade you a Bible for the rat. If you'll read it and say prayers to God, I'll take the rat."

"Why would I do that? God ain't never done nothing for me."

"He's doing something for you right now because as I said, I don't like rats. Just the same, my word is good. I'm a Christian and I don't lie. I'll not only take good care of the rat I might even make him famous. I'm a reporter." What had she done?

He wrung his hands. "All right. All right. Get me the Bible. I'll read it."

"I usually carry one with me when I'm working, but I'm on vacation." Ha. That was a joke.

The man's pleading look touched her.

"I have a Bible at my cabin. I'll bring it to you while you're in custody and arrange to get the rat. If you're lying about reading the Good Book, you'll have to answer to God, not me. He's the one who passes judgement, so if I were you, I'd give it an honest try."

The tendon in the man's neck twitched. "I will, but you have to take Little Roy now."

Emily sucked in a gasp and it created a noise similar to the rat's squeak. "I can't. I need to contact animal control…"

"No, you idiot." The man's face turned white.

Disgusted, Emily couldn't hold back a choking noise. "Not to give him to them. To get him in a cage."

The man glared at her. "You can't keep him in a cage."

"Eventually, I probably won't. First things first

though. He will have a good bath, delousing, and his shots, so calm down, and I'll make the arrangements."

"He ain't gonna' like all that, but it's better than having no one to take care of 'im." The man patted his pocket. "Did you hear that, Little Roy?"

Squeak. Squeak.

This was going to be harder than she thought. They talked to each other.

"Squeak. Squeak."

Would he even read the Bible? She'd probably never know, but it was worth a try, and after all, how long could the rat live?

Nick stood with his jaws down to his belt buckle. "Okay, enough about the rat." He sent a harsh expression to the killer. "Who are you?"

The man snarled. "Well now that's a good question. Folks call me Rough."

A blue light flashed into the yard and Nick, Rough, and Emily turned toward it.

In moments Sheriff Rivers got out of his law enforcement car and walked straight to Rough. "I'll take him now."

Nick joined him, and he shook Nick's hand. "Thank you for your help."

Rough took a step back, terror flashing in his eyes.

Emily walked to Sheriff Rivers. "He told us he was Rough? Who is he?"

"I don't know." Sheriff Rivers scowled at the man. "What's your name?"

"Like I said, my friends call me Rough."

Sheriff Rivers gave Rough, or whatever his name was, the once over. "Do they now?"

Rough nodded. That didn't stop Sheriff Rivers from

pushing through. "Okay, what's your last name, Rough?"

"I think it's Moonright, or something like that. I never knew my parents."

His words sent a sympathetic ache through Emily. "Uh, Sheriff Rivers, would you help me with something?"

"Sure, what can I do for you?"

Emily forced the words she didn't want to say over a big knot in her throat. "I need to have animal control go to the jail, meet Rough there and put his pet rat in a cage."

"Whatever for?"

"I've made a deal with Rough. He's going to read a Bible and I'm going to take care of Little Roy. I'll take the Bible to Rough tomorrow."

Rough patted his pocket. "Hear that, Little Roy?"

"Squeak. Squeak."

Nick blinked several times before he blew out a big breath and muttered. "I've seen it all now!"

Sheriff Rivers opened his mouth partway, but nothing came out of it until his Adams apple bopped a few times. "Okay, I'm going to sign off on this without asking."

Rough gave Emily a pitiful look she never imagined a murderer could have. "You ain't gonna' change your mind are 'ye."

"No, I told you. My word is good." Emily put as much reassurance in her voice as she could.

Sheriff Rivers took Rough by the arm. "Let's go." He put him in the police car and drove off."

Nick stood with his hand on the base of his neck. "Well, that's progress, but we still don't know who's running the show and what their end game is. *And…*I want to know what you're going to do with a rat." He turned and gave Emily a quick kiss. Before she had a chance to reply he said, "I'm going to follow Sheriff Rivers and find out what Rough has to say."

"Will you bring back the rat?" Emily asked, even though she didn't want the creature.

Nick snickered. "Sure. I'll take it to the office. You can get him tomorrow."

"Okay, thank you."

After Nick left, Emily went inside and sat on the sofa until she heard a racket outdoors. It sounded as though a herd of elks ran through the woods. She stood and looked out the window where light poured through the forest. After so much doubt when she first told Nick and Sheriff Rivers about the dead body, and the murderer running loose in these hills, Sheriff Rivers finally had the killer in custody. The bomb squad and hazmat team had arrived. Now if they could find the box, maybe she could get on with her vacation.

Chapter Twenty-Seven

The next morning, Emily tugged on a pair of jeans and a T-shirt and walked at a fast pace to the manager's office, a cool breeze slapping her cheeks.

Nick stood in front of the coffee maker holding a tablespoon of grounds in midair at the refreshment table.

"Hi, do you want me to do that?"

"Sure." He smiled wide then glanced at his watch. "We'll have it ready when Sheriff Rivers gets here." He directed his gaze toward the door then looked at his watch again. "Where is he?"

A gurgling sound penetrated the air

"Thanks. I need coffee more than ever today."

Emily looked over her shoulder. "Me too. It won't take long now." She scanned the office. "Where's Little Roy? Did you forget."

Nick let out a sarcastic laugh. "Oh no, he's in the manager's quarters. I'll get him for you when you're ready to leave."

With the morning pick-me-up brewed the aroma of vanilla wafted through the room as Sheriff Rivers entered.

"Hmm. That smells good."

Anxious to hear what Rough told Sheriff Rivers, Emily poured a cup and gave it to him as fast as she could. "Here ya' go."

He took the drink, set it on Nick's desk, and he and Nick sat down. Then Emily got her coffee and joined them. Nick pulled three paper towels from the holder and folded them as napkins, handing one to Sheriff Rivers and Emily. "We're sitting on thumbtacks. Tell us. What's the deal with this guy?"

Emily tapped the side of her cup.

Sheriff Rivers took a deep breath. "We aren't sure yet. Last night Rough had his jaws locked up like he had lockjaw. The bomb squad and hazmat team have gone farther into the hills, but they're still out there, so I don't know anything yet. I'll let you know what's happening as soon as I do." He gazed at Emily with a puzzled look. "This guy Rough believes you'll show up today at the jail with a Bible."

"I will." Emily tried to sound nonchalant as though she took in rats every day. "Thank you for sending animal control." She leaned back in her chair. "I hate rats, but…"

Sheriff Rivers snorted and spilled his drink. "Oops. I'm sorry."

"Don't worry. I'll take care of it." Emily reached over with her paper towel and started wiping up the mess as Nick hopped up.

He brought over the washrag, finished cleaning the spill then filled Sheriff Rivers' cup and sat back down.

"As for the Bible," Emily continued. "When I told him if he would read the Bible, I would take care of…um…the ah…Little Roy, I meant it. No one can dictate what a person believes in the depths of his being, but reading the Bible is a start. Maybe it sounds weird that I'd do Rough a favor after all that's happened." Emily pressed her lips tight. Just how strange would her comment sound to Sheriff Rivers and Nick? Oh well, there's no substitute for telling the truth. "Sometimes I have this voice inside my brain that tells me to do something because it's the right thing to do." She slapped the desk. "Now, mind you, I'm not enthusiastic about this particular message. I had to hear it a few times before I answered, but I'm convinced things will work out between me and the creature."

"Maybe Little Roy will soften your opinion of rodents, or at least one of them." Sheriff Rivers laughed. Then he gulped down his coffee and held up his cup. "Hmm. Thank you. It's what I needed to get me going. Hopefully, I can fill you in soon." He got up, pushed in his chair, gave them a thumbs up then left.

"I'll be right back." Nick went to the managers' quarters, returning with Little Roy, holding the cage out to Emily. "Be careful with this thing."

"I will. He's going to the vet before I take him to see Rough."

~

Emily carried the cage as far as she could from her body as she walked up the steps to the jailhouse. The veterinarian had told her Little Roy was a vole, showed her its clawed feet, and told her voles make good pets if they're fed the food they need. Then she had handed her a list, which included grass, tree roots, and apple peelings.

Little Roy hovered in a corner of the cage. Emily stared at his tiny ears. She guessed that was why Rough named him "Little" Roy. *A vole, huh. Still looks like a rat to me.* She strode through the metal detectors and into the lobby.

The greeter's jaw fell open when Emily and Roy stepped to the receptionist's window, a cutout with bars over it. "Hi, I'm Emily Hanover, here to see Rough Moonright."

The woman glared at Emily and Roy.

Emily shifted her weight. "Ah-hmm."

The woman scanned her computer screen, lifted her head, and blinked a few times. At last, in a calm tone as though she had accepted Emily and Little Roy, she said, "Okay, follow me."

She unlocked a heavy steel door, and they entered the area with the law breakers behind bars. Their greeter motioned to the first cell and left. Emily's stomach swirled as though someone stirred it with a stick. She would never commit a crime, if for no other reason than she couldn't stand the restrictive, trapped, hopeless sensation this environment sent coursing through her.

The rat, vole, whatever he was, hopped up and scurried to the front of the cage as Emily walked to Rough's cell. She stood for a few minutes and breathed deep. "See, he's fine. I'm keeping my word."

The rat started clawing at the cage and squeaking like crazy, so Emily placed him closer to the jail cell. Rough poked his hand between two of the bars and stuck his forefinger into the rat's cage. "Hello, Little Roy." He rubbed the top of its noodle and Little Roy settled down.

Emily passed Rough a Bible and a small, paperback devotional book. "Read these, and I promise I'll treat Little Roy like a king."

She hoped Rough agreed because every nerve in her body stood ready to get out of here.

"Hear that, Little Roy. Look what I did for you."

"No." Emily pointed her forefinger at Rough and put as much authority in her tone as she could. "You need to understand. You didn't do this for him, and I didn't do this for him. The Lord did."

Rough blinked several times, leaned his neck back, and struck a dumb-founded look.

Emily couldn't stand the jail any longer. "Start reading."

"Okay."

After she turned and left, she heard Rough calling out down the hall, "Bye, Little Roy. Bye little rat. Bye, Little Roy." She'd never been so glad to leave anywhere in her entire life. Even the cave wasn't this bad. Uh, well maybe it was, but she was happy to have left both places. She held up Little Roy's cage. "Now, to figure out how I'm going to stand you."

As if he understood her loathing, the vole hovered in the corner.

After she took Little Roy to the cabin, she looked around for a place to put him where she wouldn't see him very often. Finally, she placed him behind the sofa. It was two o'clock before she fed him and put water in his cage.

Knocks fell on the door. When she opened it, Nick strode inside.

"Hi," she said as Nick gazed about the room.

"Where's Little Roy?"

"Behind the sofa."

"Behind the sofa?" Nick peeked behind the couch. That's not a good place for a pet. I'm sure the poor thing's in some type of rat shock. He's had a bath, a delousing, and a shot, and he's penned up. At least put him where he can look at something other than the floor."

"A pet? He's not my pet. Anyway, he's better off here all cleaned up than he was nasty running around in a cave."

Nick held up his hand in rebuttal. "Not really. He's totally out of his environment."

Emily thought about how the jailhouse weirded her out. "Hmm. I see what you mean. All right, I'll move him." She scanned the room. "I'll put him on the end table."

She relocated the rodent.

Nick studied the creature. "I see you fed him and gave him water."

"Of course, my word is good. I told Rough whoever-he-is I would take care of Little Roy, and I will." Emily didn't try to tone down the irritation in her voice.

Nick walked to the cage. "Rough actually pets this thing?"

"Yeah, he just rubs his noggin."

Nick put his finger in the cage and patted Little Roy. He stood on his hind legs, looked at Nick and made soft squeaking noises.

Nick laughed. "You'll get used to him. I came by to let you know Sheriff Rivers is coming to the manager's office at four o'clock with news."

"Thanks for letting me know. I'll be there."

~

Emily sat at military attention at Nick's desk while she and Nick directed their attention to Sheriff Rivers.

"The hazmat team found uranium stored in the cave Emily fell into, but it was in the rear in an underground tunnel, where Rough must have moved it before he cleared out. He had two private airplane pilots lined up to come get it and take it to Joe in Cuba. The F.B.I.'s tracing connections between Rough, Surley, and Roggue. Rough, Roggue, and Surley knew each other growing up. The authorities believe Surley and Roggue put the uranium in the cave." Sheriff Rivers throat resonated with a low laugh. "It probably took both of them to transport it."

Sheriff Rivers pulled his brows low. "I can't recall a Moonright family, though according to Rough, he's not even sure that's his correct name. He claims a woman, Sarah Bello, who lived in the forest, fed and housed him and sent him to school. There's an old, deserted cabin out there. Could be where Rough lived. I asked around to see if anyone knew Sarah Bello. Unfortunately, no one did. I found her name in the obituary section of the June 2020, issue of the "Broken Arrow" newspaper." The sheriff drummed his fingers on the desk. "We have no way of knowing who she was. One thing we do know—Rough knows these mountains well. He lived so far back in the hills he probably could tell us about caves and waterfalls few have ever seen. That's how he managed to out-maneuver us for as long as he did."

"Wow!" Emily ran her hand through her hair. "Apparently, Little Roy's all Rough's ever had." She lowered her voice. "Something to love that loved him back."

She would keep her promise to Rough and take Little Roy to Blue Mountain along with her memories.

~

Emily folded her jeans and T-shirts and put them in the suitcase on the bed. At last, the gas shortage had ended. She would leave today. Nick was returning to college. Was Nick the right man for her, or did God send him to help her through the pain Donnie caused? Not to mention the embarrassment of getting jilted at the altar. Either way, she was grateful she met Nick. Because of him she could smile again.

If anyone asked, she would assure them Donnie probably was exactly the right husband for someone, but as far as she was concerned, God intervened and saved her from making a big mistake. She packed her socks as someone knocked on the door.

Little Roy stood with his nose against the side of the cage and cast his beady eyes toward the entrance.

When she swung it open, Nick entered, took her in his arms, and held her so tight she could hardly breathe. Then he gave her a long, passionate kiss before he let go of her. "I will miss you, but I'm not saying good-bye. I'm saying I'll see you soon."

She fought back the tears building inside her. "Are you leaving now?"

"No, I came to tell you Sheriff Rivers wants to see us around noon, but that's a great excuse to show up at your doorstep. I just…I don't want to let you go, but I'll come to Blue Mountain. They have studio rental apartments at the campus. You could come some weekends, and spring break is in April. I'll work here for two weeks at least. Maybe you could…"

Nick's words filled Emily with thankfulness. "We'll work it out. I'll miss you too."

Nick gathered her in his arms again and held her

close.

Squeak. Squeak. Squeak. Little Roy clawed at the cage and stared at Nick.

Nick went over and petted him. He made soft, squeaking noises.

Nick turned toward Emily. "You've got to pay more attention to this poor thing."

"He's walking around the cage now and I'm warming up to him." Emily puckered her mouth and pulled it to one side. "Lukewarm, very lukewarm, but I'm trying."

"I'm sure Rough is grateful you took him." Nick headed toward the door. "I've got to get back to the office. There's lots going on with the F.B.I, and the hazmat team up here, but I'll see you at noon."

~

Nick nearly skipped back to the office. Caroline would always have a place in his heart. Yet, when he thought he could never love again because he lost her, he was wrong. He loved Emily. To think, they knew each other because a murderer scared the daylights out of her. God did work in mysterious ways.

Nick pondered the joy inside him as he strode to the refreshment table. He'd watched Emily make coffee so many times, he could do it now. She wouldn't have to. He scooped grounds for the surprise flavor he bought for Emily and soon the office smelled like chocolate cake. His mouth watered as he waited for Emily and Sheriff Rivers.

When they entered at noon, Sheriff Rivers stopped and took a wide stance at the refreshment table. "Hmm. It smells wonderful in here." He directed his attention to Nick, his eyes big. "You did this?"

"Yep."

Sheriff Rivers glanced at Emily. "She's good for you."

They all laughed, and Sheriff Rivers asked, "May I?"

"Of course." Nicke pointed to the coffee pot.

After he poured their drinks, they sat down. Sheriff Rivers put his palms on the desk. "The strangest thing happened. When I went to the jail this morning, Rough wanted to talk. He said, as we knew, he grew up with Surley and Roggue. He overheard them planning to sell uranium to a Joe in Cuba. He also heard Roggue tell Surley to look for a flash drive in cabin #120 at Sky High Campground. After Surely found it, Roggue had written, Surley should follow the map and get the diamonds as his payment. Apparently, Roggue was the go-between for Joe and Surley. They found an airline ticket to Cuba in Roggue's belongings. As Rough listned to this, I surmise he saw it as his way out of poverty. He confessed to killing Surley and Roggue and finding Joe's instructions in Roggue's belongings."

"Whew." Emily leaned back in her seat.

"I asked Rough why he changed his mind about talking." Sheriff Rivers poked the tip of his forefinger on his napkin. "He held up the Bible you gave him." He looked at Emily as though he couldn't believe his words. "He said he'd been reading it. He knew it was too late to go back and not murder Surley and Roggue, but if he could tell the truth and stop a nuclear war, it was the right thing to do."

~

Emily listened with intensity to Sheriff Rivers' words. It took several seconds for the magnitude and horror of them to sink in. She squeezed her eyes shut. There would be no war, at least not this time. "Are you going back to the jail?"

"Yes, that's my job, remember?"

"Of course." Emily's cheeks heated over her faux pas as she blurted out, "I'm going to take a picture of me petting Little Roy for you to give to Rough. I'll get it to you before I leave." Rubbing that rat, vole, or whatever he was would take all the oomph she had, but she had to do it because Rough was living up to his word. She wanted him to read as much of the Bible as he could before he went to court. Even if he got the death penalty, she'd heard North Carolina had not executed anyone in a long time. He probably would live for decades and hopefully, he'd get through all of the Good Book.

"Okay, I'll deliver it for you and make sure he knows Roy's doing well. I'm going to miss you two." He glanced at Nick then Emily. "But I think I'll see more of both of you in the future. You make a good couple."

Nick grabbed Emily around the waist and hugged her, her chair scraping over the wood floor. "I agree." He grinned big as Emily nodded.

"All right, I gotta' run. There's lots happening in these hills. I don't think I've ever seen so much paperwork."

They all chuckled then Sheriff Rivers got up and Nick and Emily stood.

After Sheriff Rivers walked outside, Nick turned toward Emily. "So, you're going home to the "Blue Mountain News" and write an article for your crime section."

"Yep, and you're returning to campus?"

"Yes, but I'm graduating early. I've given some thought to opening a Private Investigator's Office in Blue Mountain. Something tells me I could get plenty of press coverage, and maybe a little help on the job." Nick laughed. "So, if you hear someone digging in the yard or stomping on your porch this spring, it's me."

Emily grabbed Nick around the neck and gave him a big hug. He lifted her off of the floor and she soared above the mountains toward the sky, floating amid the soft clouds. The peace she sought when she came here settled around her.

Epilogue

Fifteen months later

The summer sun shone in the small window in Rough's cell. He sat on the side of his bed reading the Bible when a guard built like a football linebacker walked up.

"A man, Nick, stopped by and left some things for you. There's a picture of a woman with a rat sitting on her lap."

Rough got up, reached out, and took the photo. "That's a vole."

"Well, whatever it is." The Guard handed Rough a bag. "Also, here's more of those dried apple peelings you told Sheriff Rivers you wanted." He swiped his forehead. "Oh, I almost forgot. This guy Nick sent two messages. *Him* and Emily are engaged."

Rough's face lit up. "Wonderful."

"And, they were both happy to get the photo of you in the chapel."

Rough grinned. "Yeah, Sheriff Rivers delivered that for me. Have you given your life to Jesus?"

"Geez." The guard left shaking his head.

Rough took out a piece of a dried apple peeling,

turned around, and peered into a hole in the wall. "Come on, Little Louie, I got something for you."

The End.

Watch for *Dangerous Detour,* Book Two in the Discipleship Series: Romantic Mystery and Suspense.

Four people are in the wilderness in an ice storm. Two have lost their way. One has lost his purpose, and one his lost his soul.

Two strangers, Moose, a football coach, and Ruthie, a quiet college professor, headed home for Christmas are stranded in an ice storm on a blocked road with no phone service. When they take shelter in an old cabin, they unknowingly enter a killer's hideout. Escaping under fire, they flee into a frozen forest where all of the trees, the earth and mountains look alike covered in snow. Trying to find their way out of the forest and shake the murderer, each day they dodge bullets until the temperature drops and the world turns quiet. As Moose and Ruthie set up camps in the wilderness, they ignore the chemistry between them until each of them suffers a frightening injury. They finally pin their hopes of survival on a house Ruthie sees, but who will they find there? A friend or another foe?

www.ingramcontent.com/pod-product-compliance
Lightning Source LLC
Chambersburg PA
CBHW070419310726
48977CB00003B/753